The Christmas Wish Knotts

by

Avis M. Adams

Christmas Cookies Series

The Christmas Wish Knotts

COPYRIGHT © 2022 by Avis Marie Adams

Cover Art by *Tina Lynn Stout*

The Wild Rose Press, Inc.
PO Box 708
Adams Basin, NY 14410-0708
Visit us at www.thewildrosepress.com

Publishing History
First Edition, 2022
Trade Paperback ISBN 978-1-5092-4264-1
Digital ISBN 978-1-5092-4263-4

Christmas Cookies Series
Published in the United States of America

Sif dropped her bouquet. "This is all my fault. If only I…"

"None of this is your fault." Nanc took her hands and gripped them. "Look at me. He did this. Not you. We'll see him in court."

"What will I do with two hundred Wedding Knotts?" Sif rubbed her eyes, trying not to smear her mascara. Wait. Who cared about mascara?

"Send them to Boris's family?" Dad shrugged. "I thought it was odd when they didn't show."

Her mom brushed a strand of hair from Sif's face. "I never liked him, by the way."

"But…" Sif couldn't believe her ears. "Why didn't you say something?"

"I did, but you didn't listen." She took Sif by the shoulders. "This is for the best. I know it doesn't seem like it, but—"

"This time, I have to agree with your mom. He wasn't good enough for you." Dad pulled her into a bear hug.

"I'm going to announce the banquet is still on." Mom headed for the door, blowing a kiss before disappearing out the door.

Sif leaned into Dad's broad chest. She took a deep breath. She just wanted to curl against Daddy and let him hold her forever, but she couldn't let Boris have the final word. She'd show him and all her friends. She'd be fine. "No, you're right. I'm okay." She grinned as her stomach tied into a knot. "Let's do this."

"That's my girl." Dad held her at arm's length and smiled.

Other Wild Rose Press Titles by Avis M. Adams:

The Incident

Dedication

To the real Nanc and Mr. Martini!

Chapter 1

The Wedding Debacle

Voices echoed in Seattle's Grand Lodge. She stood under an arching trellis of yellow roses. Their sweet aroma clogged Sif's nostrils until her head pounded, and she gripped her bouquet like a dagger. Nanc stood with her at the trellis and adjusted her train for the twentieth time. Every seat on her side of the lodge was filled. The whispering and head nods paralyzed her.

Pastor Jim walked down the aisle, but the music had droned on for so long the pianist had switched to light jazz. She glanced at the pastor, and he shrugged.

"It's been fifty-four minutes, Sif," Pastor Jim whispered.

She peeked over her shoulder at her best friend and maid of honor. Nanc shook her head and put a hand on Sif's shoulder.

He wasn't coming.

Pastor folded the book of vows in his hands, the sky-blue ribbons she'd bound them with wrapping around his wrist.

It wasn't fair. Sunlight shone through the window. She'd gotten good weather, only to have Boris jilt her? Not even a text, nothing.

"What do I do? I don't know what to do. I mean…" Her voice quavered, and tears sprang to her eyes. She was drowning.

"Head to the dressing room," he said, nudging her toward the open door to the right of the arch. "I'll make an announcement."

What did he need to announce? Wasn't it obvious? Her vision blurred as she dashed to the door, her wedding dress rustling. This couldn't be happening. There was still time for Boris to show up and take her hand...

Pastor's voice echoed in the lodge. "I'm sorry, friends, but the wed—"

She slammed the door, drowning out Pastor's voice, leaned against the wall, and sobbed. Tears rolled down her cheeks, leaving dark splotches on her cream satin gown. Nanc burst into the room.

"We're going to sue that jerk." Nanc paced the room, shredding the white roses in her bouquet.

"What?" Sif sank to the floor and blew her nose. "Where could he be, Nanc?"

"Good riddance, is all I can say." Nanc ran her hand through her short hair.

"I spent so much time planning this wedding and baking my Wedding Knotts. I thought they'd bring me luck."

"Hey." Nanc knelt and took Sif's hands in hers. "It's all going to be fine. We'll just rename them Good Luck Knotts because you're lucky he's gone."

Sif choked on her sob. "I don't feel lucky."

"He was never good enough for you." Nanc glared at the door. "Listen, we can still have the banquet, and I want one of those Good Luck Knotts. We fete, then we sue."

"I don't think..." Sif wiped her eyes. "What are

you saying? I can't go out there. Everyone knows he bailed on me." Sif laid her cheek against the wall.

Nanc sat beside her and put her arm around Sif's shoulder. Sif sighed. What would she do without Nanc? She pressed her cheek against her friend's warm shoulder. Maybe she'd absorb some of Nanc's confidence because this had drained her.

Nanc jumped to her feet. "I have a plan. Have you ever heard of the Breach of Promise to Marry?"

"What? No." Sif groaned. She didn't want to think about promises right now. "What is it?"

"I have to do more research, of course, but he left you at the altar, after you've paid for the reception and bought a condo together. We have to protect your investment in a life that isn't going to happen anymore, at the very least you should get the condo."

Sif wiped her nose on her sleeve. "Oh, Nanc, I can't think of that right now."

"That's why you have me." Nanc put her arm around Sif.

"I've been too busy to notice anything, between hiring photographers and baking cookies…" She pressed her fists to her chest. "I can hardly breathe. Why didn't I see this coming?"

Nanc helped her to her feet. "This is not your fault. Boris did this, and where's Shirley? Isn't the wedding planner supposed to be at the wedding?"

Where was Shirley? Sif's stomach rolled, and her dress crinkled as she pressed her hands over her tummy. Her mind raced with images of Boris smiling at Shirley, winking at her, and Shirley giggling in annoying snorts. "Shirley?"

"I never liked her either. Here, let's get this veil

off. Tissue?" Nanc dabbed at Sif's face. "There. That's better."

Sif grabbed Nanc's hands. "I should have seen the signs. He never intended to go through with this wedding. I'm such a fool." She sobbed into the tissue Nanc handed her.

"He's going to pay, don't worry." Nanc paced the room, her hands clenched.

Sif didn't want to make him pay. She wanted to marry him. How would she recover from this debacle?

The door opened, and her mom slipped in. "Oh, honey." She rushed to Sif, crushing her in a hug.

"Mom." Sif fell against her. "What am I going to do?"

Mom held Sif's face in her hands. "You are going to show everyone how strong and beautiful you are. Besides, Aunt Darlene came two thousand miles for a wedding feast and some of your Wedding Knotts. I say we party."

Nanc stood, hands on her hips. "I like that plan, and we're calling them Good Luck Knotts now."

Sif shook her head. "I can't face all those people."

The door opened again. Her dad filled the door, his fists shaking. "I'll kill him."

"Harold, that's not helping." Mom glared at him.

Sif dropped her bouquet. "This is all my fault. If only I…"

"None of this is your fault." Nanc took her hands and gripped them. "Look at me. He did this. Not you. We'll see him in court."

"What will I do with two hundred Wedding Knotts?" Sif rubbed her eyes, trying not to smear her mascara. Wait. Who cared about mascara?

"Send them to Boris's family?" Dad shrugged. "I thought it was odd when they didn't show."

Her mom brushed a strand of hair from Sif's face. "I never liked him, by the way."

"But…" Sif couldn't believe her ears. "Why didn't you say something?"

"I did, but you didn't listen." She took Sif by the shoulders. "This is for the best. I know it doesn't seem like it, but—"

"This time, I have to agree with your mom. He wasn't good enough for you." Dad pulled her into a bear hug.

"I'm going to announce the banquet is still on." Mom headed for the door, blowing a kiss before disappearing out the door.

Sif leaned into Dad's broad chest. She took a deep breath. She just wanted to curl against Daddy and let him hold her forever, but she couldn't let Boris have the final word.

She'd show him and all her friends. She'd be fine. "No, you're right. I'm okay." She grinned as her stomach tied into a knot. "Let's do this."

"That's my girl." Dad held her at arm's length and smiled.

She nodded, and a sob escaped. She put a hand over her mouth. He frowned, and she sighed and patted his hands. *Pull yourself together, Sif. He'll worry until he sees you eat something.*

She turned to her best friend. "Nanc, can you help me out of this stupid dress?"

Nanc nodded. "Now you're talking."

Dad brushed her cheek with his hand before he left, and Sif reached for her bouquet on the floor. She pushed her nose into the roses.

"This has been the wedding debacle of the century." She tossed the bouquet onto a table and frowned at Nanc. Could she do this? "Maybe if I pretend it's just a family reunion?"

Nanc grinned and unzipped the dress, and Sif stepped out of the cream satin fluff.

Chapter 2

A New Tenant

A stiff breeze pushed Sif along the pier as she sprinted the last one hundred feet to the last board where the wooden planks ended, and the cement sidewalk began. She sprang onto the concrete, her step light and swift, then jogged across the street to the parking lot of the Cliff Edge Condos. She'd need an extra-long cooldown after that run. She tucked loose ponytailed hairs behind her ear, the November breeze invigorating and cool.

Gravel crunched under tires. Who would be driving into the lot now? A man behind the wheel of a red Camry scanned the lot for an empty space.

There went her long cooldown. Sweat dripped down her back. She was a mess. Yep, shower time. She rushed to the back door and reached for the handle, but the door pushed open, and Elgin stepped through.

"Oh, there you are. I have someone I want you to meet." Elgin leaned heavily on his cane and took her right arm. "Did you have a good run?"

Sif gritted her teeth through her smile. He was up to something. Ugh. Who could he want her to meet, and what kind of friend would make her meet someone looking like this? She sighed. It was too late to escape now. The Camry backed into a parking spot.

"This might be my new tenant." Elgin winked at

her. "With any luck." He limped toward the sedan.

"New tenant? You're having knee surgery, not moving out, right?" She couldn't lose Elgin. He was the only one who could keep the Cliff Edge Condo drama to a minimum. She tagged behind him as he hobbled across the lot to the car.

She ran her hand over her lumpy hair. "Elgin—I need a shower."

Elgin turned. "You look ravishing, with that rosy complexion. Come on. Let's get this over with."

Elgin raised a hand in greeting as a young man stepped out of the car. He stood, tall and disheveled, his hair dark and windblown, a tuft falling over his forehead.

If she'd only been two seconds faster, she could have avoided all of this. She glanced up at the man and blinked. His eyes were deep, brown pools of warmth, and his smile melted her. Sif tucked a loose strand of her hair behind her ear and gulped.

She wasn't ready for Mr. Good-Looking. Her pulse pounded. She hadn't even recovered from her run yet. She inhaled and blew out a long, slow breath, a trick she'd learned in yoga. He closed the distance between them in three steps and held his hand out to Elgin, but his gaze was on her. Who was this guy?

Get a grip. It's just a prospective tenant. But why does he have to be so cute?

"You must be Elgin. Nice to finally meet you." He shook Elgin's hand and then gestured to the building. "I love the vintage architecture. What is it? 1920s?"

"Close." Elgin's chest expanded as he clasped the man's hand. He owned the building and took pride in showing it off. "1922, to be exact."

Sif rubbed her sweaty palms on her thermal running pants. Maybe if she didn't move, he would forget she was there. She took a step back.

"I didn't think I'd find anything with a three-month lease, so this is perfect." He gazed across the lot to the Puget Sound. "I can't wait to see the view."

Three months? That wouldn't give him long enough to be a problem. Sif rolled her shoulders, but she frowned at Elgin. How had he talked her into this? Seagulls cried outside, and a giant cloud billowed in the shape of a dinosaur over the Olympic Mountains.

"It was meant to be," Elgin said.

That was it? This guy had passed the Elgin test already?

"May I introduce Sif. She lives on the third floor. Always pays before the first."

Sif did a double take. Was that how he thought of his tenants, by when they paid their rent? Elgin grinned, oblivious to her reaction. She held out her hand.

"Nice to meet you, Roger." His warm, large hand engulfed hers, and a jolt tingled up her arm. She pulled away and took a step back. He had the build of a runner, lean and tall. His eyes sparkled as he smiled at her. She took another step back, as the tingle intensified. She hadn't tingled since before the wedding debacle, but she didn't want tingles. Did she? She had just gotten to the point where she didn't think about Boris every day. This was the last thing she needed.

Elgin tapped his cane on the floor. "Earth to Sif."

Sif shook her head and closed her mouth. How long had it been hanging open?

"Roger is a hospitalist, whatever that is." Elgin chuckled and shifted from one foot to the other. His bad knee must be acting up.

Sif put out a hand to steady him. Good thing his surgery was soon.

Roger ran his fingers through his hair and inhaled in preparation to explain his job, which he probably had to do ad nauseam. "It just means I work with patients during their hospital stay, coordinating care, checking test results, stuff like that, but I'm only here until they fill the position." His gaze burned into her.

"That's nice." She cringed. Nice? Really?

How did he manage to make a mundane job description sound sexy? She glanced at the door. If he caught a whiff of her, this would be their first and last meeting. "Well, it was nice meeting you, but I better go."

"Nice to meet you, too," Roger called as she dashed to the door, waving over her shoulder.

"She's just finished a five-miler, you know," Elgin said. "I used to run with her, until my knee went bone on bone, but enough of that."

He cleared his throat. "Let's start with the building. It has fifteen units on three floors—" The door shut behind her, cutting off the echo of Elgin's spiel.

She jogged up the three flights to her condo, unlocked her door with trembling fingers, and rushed inside. The dark entry enveloped her with warmth as she kicked off her running shoes and padded down the hall to the living room. She still tingled from Roger's large hand enveloping hers. What was it about this guy? He was good-looking, but so was Boris. She pressed a hand to her chest to slow her heart rate.

Visions of Shirley and Boris in Barbados slammed her all over again, and her chest constricted. She didn't need this. But why did all the old pain return so easily? Roger didn't even resemble Boris. She paused and took in the view. Puget Sound with Vashon and Maury Islands and behind them the Olympics, white and majestic, the million-dollar view that had sold her and Boris on this unit.

She clenched her shaking fist. Why did it always come back to Boris? All men were not like Boris, were they? She sighed. Still, after fourteen months, she couldn't meet a new guy without running away. Damn Boris.

Mr. Martini rubbed against her leg. She scooped him into her arms and gazed across the water to the mountains. Boris should be in the kitchen making a sandwich and popping open a bottle of beer. *Quit it. He's gone, and you hate him.*

No. I don't.

Martini purred, the warmth of his body soothing. "Did I tell you we have a new guy in the building, Martini? Don't worry." She buried her face in Martini's fur, then glanced out at the water. "You are my one true love."

The glint of the sun on the waves mesmerized her. She should hate Boris, but she still grieved for what could have been. "I guess it was never meant to be, Mr. Martini." She buried her face in the cat's fur.

****

Sif balanced two tins of Friendship Knott cookies in her arms and walked down the short hall that led out onto a covered porch that ran the length of the street side of the building. The Cliff Edge Condos were famous for its Christmas light display. The day after Thanksgiving, workers wove the lights around each post of the intricate architecture.

The porch was also the perfect place to eavesdrop on neighbors. She'd found that out the hard way after a tear-filled conversation with Nanc, but all was quiet now. She trotted down the stairs, her hair bouncing with each step. Nothing like a long hot shower after a run.

The sign on the noticeboard said Poker Game: 7:00 p.m., Club Room. She still had time to make it. The card game would end at 9:00 p.m. sharp. Early evenings worked best for her these days. Insomnia hit soon after the—

Don't go there.

She pulled her phone from her pocket. 6:48. She had time to call Mom. She hit speed dial and leaned against the wall of mailboxes. Saturday night. Cookies and cards with the Quatre Hens and a call to Mom? She shook her head. It had been fourteen months since Boris had—

Her shoulders slumped. She should be out at the with Nanc, but something about loud music and laughter turned her stomach.

"Rechannel that negative energy," her therapist had said. "Focus on your new condo, teaching, running." Good advice, but it should be. She paid enough for it. Mom's phone rang and rang. She must be in the barn. Sif didn't leave a message. What would she say? She didn't have enough energy to rechannel anything after Boris.

She rubbed her temple. It wasn't too late to turn back. Nanc's invitation to the Village Public House was still good. She could wear her little black dress and...

No. She couldn't spend one more Saturday pretending to smile. Avoiding all the guys. Refusing to dance. And there was always someone who'd ask, "How are you?" with a wrinkled brow and a thin-lipped smile. What a stupid question. She was fine, wasn't she? She had to be fine.

But she wasn't fine.

She pulled out her phone and dialed Mom again. It went straight to voicemail again. "Mom, I haven't seen you in six months. This is ridiculous. Leave the sheep for one weekend, please. I miss you." Those sheep had replaced her in her mother's heart.

She juggled two cookie tins filled with knotts in her arms. Her go-to cookies had gone from Wedding Knotts to Good Luck Knotts, then to Friendship Knotts. She got her passion for cookies from her cookie-baking great-grandmother, but when had she turned into her grandmother? Baking was how she rechanneled her energy, not that her therapist approved. "Be with other people. Get out there and socialize."

She would stop by Elgin's after the card game and see how he was doing before surgery then give him his cookie tin. She'd loaded it with all his favorites: spritz, butterscotch balls, and Friendship Knotts. Maybe they'd take his mind off his upcoming surgery. He seemed nervous, but that was normal, right?

She slowed by his door. His voice blended with another. Was Roger still here? She couldn't make out details. She leaned in closer. Laughter must mean Roger got the sublet. He was so...so...so...what? Young? And his hair and teeth? He was too perfect. She shook her head. Boris had dubbed the eavesdropping and behind-doors scenes "Cliff Edge Condo drama." But what had pushed him into Shirley's arms? Sif enjoyed drama. It distracted her from her own.

13

Trudy's rolled *r*'s stopped Sif's progression outside the club room. She only reverted to French when she was angry about something. But what was she angry about tonight? Drama. Sif leaned against the doorframe.

"Our poor Sifjar, getting left at the altar, and now Elgin does this." Trudy was the only one who used her full name. This was going to be interesting. She glanced down the hall. The last thing she needed was to get caught eavesdropping.

"I agree. She's lived here fourteen months, and don't get me wrong. I love her, but all she does is mope around her condo." Linda banged on the table.

"She's not ready for someone new. She never sleeps. Just last night, she was on the porch at two a.m. going for another run." Ellen must have been talking with her neighbor Mr. DeVoss again.

"And why does she want to hang out with four old hens like us every Saturday? I mean, she doesn't even play cards." Linda again, of course.

"It's the wedding diablo," Trudy said.

"Debacle, dear." Mabel's calm voice broke into Trudy's high-pitched one. Good old Mabel was always on her side. Besides, going for runs was normal, right?

"That's what I said." Trudy snorted.

Sif clutched the box of cookies, tears burning the back of her eyes. Did they always talk about her? When had that started? She opened the box, picked up a spritz but put it back. This batch had gluten, and she hadn't taken her pill. That's all she needed, diarrhea to go with the pity.

"I wouldn't spend two seconds moping around over Boris, that rat. She's thirty-six. Tick tock, time's a-wasting."

Thirty-six? What? She clutched the cookie tin. Her nose itched from her sweater fuzz, and she wiped it on the back of her sleeve.

"She's only twenty-nine." Thank heavens for Mabel.

She glanced at her outfit, bulky sweater, faded jeans, and stained slippers. She did need a makeover. She stifled a sneeze but squeezed the cookie tin, and the lip popped open. A butterscotch ball plopped onto the floor and rolled into the club room.

She couldn't let them say another word, and snatching up the butterscotch ball, threw it into the laurel hedge and strode into the room.

"Oh, look who's here." Mabel patted the chair beside her, a grin on her pudgy face.

She could always count on Mabel. "Thank you." She smiled as she settled in the empty chair next to her.

Mabel had always been her champion with the other Quatre Hens. They didn't want to add a fifth, but Mabel said they needed a young chick in the group. They agreed but still didn't fully accept her.

She had more in common with Mabel who had been an English teacher at the local high school. She still grieved her husband who had died of cancer five years ago. She'd sat with Sif and cried with her those first days after the wedding debacle. Sif had found a kindred spirit. Someone who understood Shakespeare and the rewards of teaching, as well as the exhaustion of grieving.

She glared at Linda. Thirty-six, my butt. *Hmph.* The green felt card table sat in the middle of the room, the picture window showcasing Puget Sound a welcome sight.

Linda nodded at Sif and passed two cards to Trudy. Ellen got one card, and Mabel three. Linda placed two cards in front of herself, and the playing continued.

"Sif, you'll have to sit this one out." Linda put her cards face down on the table. "We're in the middle of our first hand."

****

The Quatre Hens sat at the card table, the felt muffling the cards as they hit the table. Trudy and Mabel were hot tonight, but Sif couldn't keep her eyes open. She arranged a plate with Friendship Knotts and left it on the side table for them and stifled a yawn as she slogged down the hall.

A light shone under Elgin's door. She'd better drop off his tin. She knocked, and he opened the door. "Sif." He grinned and led her into the immaculate living room. The peekaboo view of Puget Sound spread out before her, tall fir trees framing the scene.

She'd cried at the sight of this view the day she moved into the condo without Boris. She'd vowed not to cry for him, not when she had this view to rejuvenate her. She sank into a matching wingback chair across from Elgin.

"So, you check into the hospital tomorrow morning?" Sif handed him the smaller tin of cookies.

"Thank you." He grinned, taking the tin from her. "Yes, I do. Roger moves in tomorrow, and after surgery and recovery, I'll go from the hospital to my daughter's home after they clear me, of course. I can't wait to get a new knee." He shook the tin. "I might leave a few of these for Roger if he's lucky. By the way, what did you think?" Elgin beamed.

Really? Was he a matchmaker now? She wouldn't

make this easy for him. "Think of what?"

He laughed and shook his head. "Of Roger, of course. He's going to need a friend, someone to stick up for him against the Quatre Hens."

He was matchmaking. "He looked like he could stick up for himself."

"The Hens went a little long in their poker game tonight, didn't they?"

"Trudy is holding on for the final win, so she couldn't let anyone leave, but I couldn't keep my eyes open a minute longer."

Elgin scoffed, and Sif sank deeper into the chair. Here it comes. The "Why are you hanging out with old ladies who won't even let you play cards with them?" speech.

"They love your company, I'm sure, but wouldn't—"

"Oh, look at the time." Sif rose from the chair. "I have a long drive tomorrow."

"Going to your mom's?" Elgin sat back and rubbed his sore knee.

"Yes. If Mohamed won't come to the mountain—" Sif scooted onto the edge of the chair. "Why are they checking you in on a Sunday? Is it your heart?"

Elgin nodded with a grimace. "I'm seventy-eight, remember? They have to check my ticker to make sure I survive so they can torture me with physical therapy."

He'd be fine, right? He had to be. He grinned at her, and she chuckled, rising from the chair. She held out her hand, and he swatted it away, pulling her into a hug that almost toppled her into his lap.

"Oh, Elgin."

"If I were twenty years younger, I'd give Roger a

run for his money. You'd be in big trouble, missy." He growled at her, and she laughed.

"So would you." She kissed his forehead. "I'll see myself out." She waved from the door, the view behind Elgin drawing her gaze.

Lights from the pier gleamed off the water like crystals. She'd take this view over Boris any day.

Chapter 3

Damn Boris

Whitecaps frothed on Puget Sound, and the water rolled with the passing of a cargo ship. Sif sat in an overstuffed chair, gazing out the large window, Mr. Martini in her lap. She brushed her tears away and sniffed. All it took was a gray day, and she couldn't stop her own waterworks. Plus, Linda thought she was thirty-six? What the heck. Linda had always been her biggest critic of all the Quatre Hens. A lamp cast its golden reflection on the window, along with her swollen eyes and pouty lips. Her tears fall harder. She'd settle for thirty-six because she looked forty-six. She plucked a fuzz ball from her sweater.

What was it about watching a bunch of old ladies play poker on Saturday night that captivated her so? It was safe, that was for sure, and Mabel's smile drew her in like a huge hug. She didn't get that from her own mother these days, what with the new sheep on the farm and all the pregnant ewes.

Another Sunday alone in her favorite chair. How had she slipped into this rut?

Damn Boris.

Sif shuddered. Had she always been this lonely? Boris had saved her from this in college. She'd sleepwalked from class to class, until Boris sank into a chair beside her in the library and asked her one question.

"What are you reading?"

She'd put the book down and followed him into his life. He gave her a sense of belonging, a butterflies-in-the-stomach lightness. Was it his bright smile or his shimmering blue eyes? That's probably what drew Shirley to him, like a moth to a flame.

Damn Shirley.

Sif grabbed a cookie from the tin and held it for the cat, who nibbled.

"You love my Friendship Knotts, don't you, Martini?"

The cat purred and kneaded her leg.

She pulled Mr. Martini into her lap. "Maybe we should rename these cookies for Christmas. What do you think of Christmas Wish Knotts?" She stroked the cat, and he purred louder.

"Should we make a wish to make the name change official?" But what would she wish for? True love? No. True love was a myth. She nibbled on the cookie, and a burst of orange filled her mouth. Maybe the universe would. make the wish for her?

Martini meowed as a cargo ship cruised by headed south, leaving a wake a half-mile long through the whitecaps. Its lights flashed, and the colored boxcars floated down the Sound to the port of Tacoma. Twilight on a late autumn evening with lights glistening over the water was one of her favorite times, even in the rain. She sighed and sank farther into the chair.

She pulled a tissue from the box and dabbed her eyes. She should be sharing this view with Boris, but here she sat, alone with her cat, in this frumpy sweater.

Why couldn't she move on?

Was it the humiliation? Damn Shirley. Worst wedding planner ever. She should have confronted Shirley when she'd started calling Boris with her wedding questions. She should have asked Boris why his business trips kept him overnight, and why he never called when he was away. She'd been so happy and so busy doing Shirley's job she didn't see all the red flags. She'd been blind.

But why did he let the wedding plans go on? All her friends and family witnessed his betrayal. She opened the text he'd sent ten minutes before the wedding. The text she was too busy to open. Why hadn't she checked her phone? It would have saved her the humiliation of standing there, waiting…

"Sorry, babe. I hope you can forgive me someday."

Instead, she'd climbed to the gallery to watch people as they were ushered in. But his friends and family never came. That should have been her first clue.

She cleared her throat and stroked the cat. One day she'd have to break the pattern of sitting in this chair crying over that day. The phone rang, and she jumped. She wiped her eyes and fumbled for her phone. Nanc.

"Hey, I was wondering if I'd hear from you today." She ran her hand over Martini's soft fur.

"Just checking in. How you doin'? I know how you get on these cold, gray days."

"I'm fine. Spent last night with the Quatre Hens." Sif hit Speaker and hugged Martini to her chest. He licked her face.

Nanc snorted. "Of course, you did. So, are they your new Saturday night party friends?"

"No, silly."

21

"Why do they call themselves the Cat Hens? I mean, it makes sense if they love them some cats, but do they?"

"It's not cat, silly. It's *quatre*. You know, like four in French."

"Fine, *quatre*. But why do you spend so much time with them? I missed you last night." Nanc's sigh hung heavy in the phone.

"I know." Sif wiped her eyes with her sleeve. She pressed her fingers to her temple. Nanc was really putting the pressure on. Would she lose her best friend because of Boris?

****

She woke with a start, Martini asleep in her lap. She'd done it again, drifted into sleep while crying in this stupid chair. She had to stop obsessing over Boris and that horrible day. She stood, placing the cat on the floor, and trudged into the kitchen. A nice cup of chamomile tea would help.

She glanced at the clock, 2:43 a.m. Martini meowed.

"It's not time for breakfast yet, mister." She ruffled his fur, then glanced out the window. No rain. She could go for a run and get back to catch some sleep.

The running lights of a boat bobbed as it motored out of the marina. Who would be leaving at this time of night? The lone boat swayed around the jetty and into open water. She sighed, and wrapping her fingers around the warm mug, she shuffled to her bedroom. She wasn't the only sleepless person in town.

Chapter 4

The Collision

Sif tied her running shoes and slipped out the door, careful not to let it slam. The last thing she wanted was a 3:00 a.m. discussion on exoskeletons of Bivalvia with Mr. DeVoss. That was a day to remember. Did he never sleep? Of course, she was one to talk. She speed-walked down the porch and opened the back door to the parking lot.

A full moon hung in the dark sky, and a car door opened. Sif jumped. It was Roger. Dang. He towered over his Toyota, slipping into his jacket, then reached in to grab his coat and bag. If she hurried, maybe she could sneak by without being noticed.

"Kind of late for a run, isn't it?"

Dang.

She spun around. "Oh, hi, again."

"Sif, right?" He held out his hand, and she took it, but he didn't let go. His hand was warm, and she stood, heart pounding as though she'd sprinted a mile. "Where'd you get a name like Sif?"

She got that question a lot. "I'm Norwegian, and Sif is short for Sifjar, kind of a family thing. I'm named after Thor's wife. She was a goddess. It also means bride, depending on your source." She gently pulled her hand from his. Source? Was she teaching a class? She ran her hand over her hair. She was going to have to start brushing it.

"Little late for a run."

"Insomnia." She shrugged. "I'm hoping it will tire me out so I can sleep a couple hours before I have to teach in the morning."

"You know I am a doctor, right?" He put his hand in his pocket and jangled his keys. "I recommend melatonin to all my patients for sleep problems."

"Oh, no. I hate taking pills, but thanks." She turned to leave, but he kept talking.

"It's dark. Where do you run?" He scanned the pier that bordered the marina, then back at her. "Is it safe out there this late at night?"

She glanced at him. "This is Village Pier Park. People are fishing at all hours, so it's very safe. Don't worry about me. I do this all the time." Did he care, or was he just bossy? She cocked a hip, waiting for him to answer.

"Okay. Forgive me, I'm not from this area, so I didn't know." He shrugged his shoulders.

"Well, I better get going. Nice to see you again." She nodded to him and ran across the street.

Was he watching her butt as she ran? Why did she care? Hmm. Good question. Did she care? This run was never going to work if she didn't stop thinking about Roger. Sif dodged a group of fishermen as she sprinted to the end of the pier.

****

The morning light made her squint as she walked down the porch. Sunshine should lift her spirits, right? Sif stumbled down a flight of stairs to the mailboxes. She rubbed the sleep from her eyes. "Ow." Now they stung. She clamped her eyes shut as she rounded the corner and ran into something solid. Was that Old Spice?

"Excuse—"

"Sif the goddess-bride, right? Did you catch up on your sleep?"

Roger? Again, and he remembered the goddess comment? Heat rose from her neck to her forehead. The deep brown pools of his eyes drew her in like a thirsty woman.

He'd gotten the same amount of sleep and look at him. Why weren't his eyes red? Pressed slacks, crisp white shirt to match his smile. She was drawn to him for sure and wanted the solid muscles of his chest under her fingers.

She shook her head and slipped the key into her mailbox and opened the door.

"I did not sleep. I'm afraid it's going to be a long day for me." She pulled out several envelopes, gazing at the addresses, but they were a blur.

"Sorry. I know all too well what that's like. Well, I better get to the hospital." He gave a nod and trotted down the stairs, his keys jingling in his pocket.

She scoffed. "Off to the hospital." Was he trying to impress her? She was, though. Impressed, that is, but still. She needed more coffee.

She pulled out the rest of her mail, two bills. A postcard fell to the floor. It was from Spokane. She grinned at the picture of a turkey waving a knife and held it to her chest. An invitation to Christmas from her sister, her favorite excuse to bake cookies she couldn't eat.

Gluten intolerance be damned. This year she would splurge and suffer in gut-cramping bliss, but she couldn't afford to travel this year. Next year she'd hand-deliver her cookies.

She stuffed her mail in her book tote and buttoned her jacket. Her phone vibrated.

"Nanc, hey." She hit speaker and opened her car door, slinging her tote onto the passenger seat.

"So, I hear there's a new guy in your building," Nanc said.

"Who told you that?"

"I have my sources."

"Okay, yes, there's a new guy in the building." Sif held the phone out and glared.

"Is he under seventy?"

"What kind of question is that? Yes, he's a doctor, a hospitalist. Kind of a temporary gig for him right now, I think."

"What's a hospitalist?"

"I'm not really sure, but he's tall, with hazel eyes, and…" Sif sank into the seat.

"Whoa, slow down."

"Hey, wasn't it you who said I needed to start looking again?" She fastened her seat belt and started her car. Her phone synced with the car broadcasting Nanc's voice.

"Yeah, well, you know what I mean. So, is he Mr. Perfect?"

"Geez. No, he's far from perfect. He does this annoying thing with his keys. He jangles them in his pocket like my creepy Uncle Stori." She snorted and adjusted the volume down.

"Uncle Stori? What is it with your family and names?"

"Quit making fun of us, or I'll think up a

Norwegian nickname for you."

"Make it sexy, and I won't mind." Nanc's laughter filled the car.

"Gotta go. I don't want to be late for class."

She put her car in reverse.

"Be careful, friend."

"No need to yell."

"I mean it, Sif. What do you even know about this guy?"

"After all the times you told me to put myself out there, and this is what you say now? You sound like my grandmother." Sif glanced over her shoulder and backed out of her parking spot. "I was born careful." Sif opened her window as she sped out of the lot, the seagulls squawking overhead.

"I worry about you, so quit complaining."

Sif laughed. "I'm not complaining, but I really have to go. I'm filling in for Vic's class this morning, and I don't want to be late."

"I want updates."

She nodded. "I'll call you tonight."

****

Sif had been teaching Shakespeare since Boris had proposed. Her favorite was *Romeo and Juliet*, and she had an easy lesson for those days after she'd had a sleepless night. She'd start with a question. "Is *Romeo and Juliet* a romance or a tragedy?"

Someone always wanted the play to be a romance, but the death of the lovers made it a tragedy every time. Students always surprised her with their passion for that play, and she didn't have to work very hard to keep the discussion going.

Once a student asked, "Did Shakespeare eat

cookies?" Probably because they knew how much she loved to bake cookies, but her blank stare made them laugh.

"Of course, Shakespeare ate cookies."

But did he? She went to her office after class and did some research on cookies in the fifteenth century and found "Knotts." She'd stayed up all night baking, and the licorice scent of caraway filled her kitchen. She rolled the dough and tied it into knots. Shakespeare must have eaten these knotts.

The first time she shared the recipe with her students surprised her as well.

Take a pound of flower and halfe a pound of shuger and ½ pound of butter and 2 whits and one yealke of Egg

They laughed at "shuger" and "yealke," which led to a lesson on the *OED, Oxford English Dictionary*, which never failed to surprise. How was it that English didn't even have a dictionary until the 1920s?

She always ended the class with cookies, something she'd do every day if she could, but nothing made her happier than bringing Shakespeare alive.

She zested an orange and added it to the dough, kneading it until blended. The aroma of fresh orange peel filled her kitchen. The timer went off, and she pulled a tray from the oven, the rich butter aroma filling the air.

Shakespeare's Knotts had become Wedding Knotts and, after Boris, Good Luck Knotts. It had become a game, and she and Nanc changed the cookie name to suit the season or the mood, Rainy Day Knotts, Lucky Knotts.

"Damn Boris," she muttered.

She pinched off a ball of dough and rolled it into a rope. Wedding Knotts were heart shaped with a twist at the bottom. Lucky Knotts were a loop with a simple twist at the bottom. This batch were actual knots, and one by one, she placed the little mounds of dough on the cookie sheet. A frantic knock at the door pulled her away from her baking. She wiped her hands on a towel. Whoever it was pounded again.

"Who is it, Martini?" She left the cookie sheet on the counter instead of putting it in the oven. Something about that knock bothered her. She glanced at the clock: 9:56 p.m. Bedtime was 9:00 p.m. for most of the *Quatre* Hens and other neighbors. She pulled the door open. Linda shifted from foot to foot, wringing her hands.

"It's Mabel." Linda glanced from Sif to the porch.

"Mabel?" Sif clutched the doorframe for support. "What's wrong?"

Linda grabbed Sif's hand and pulled her into the hallway. "She isn't answering her phone, and I know she's home. Her TV is blaring. I tried her door, but it's locked. She needs help."

Not Mabel. She couldn't lose her, and not at Christmas time. She raced after Linda down the porch to Mabel's, pulling her phone from her pocket and dialing 911 as she ran. *Hang in there, Mabel.*

"Yes. We have a woman in her eighties. She's not answering her phone or door, and her TV is on. She could be hurt. We need help."

"What is your location, ma'am?"

"The Cliff Edge Condos at 2268 Cliff House Road."

"Stay on the line, ma'am. I have a unit en route."

She tried Mabel's door. Linda was right. It was locked.

"I told you. And her TV is blaring. She's in there hurt, I just know it." Linda put her hands to her face.

Sif held the phone in one hand and grabbed Linda's hand in the other. The siren started at the top of the hill and got louder as it came. Linda covered her ears as the EMTs drove down the winding road and stopped in front of the condos.

"No Elgin." Linda gasped. "The front door's locked." Linda dashed down the porch to let them in.

Sif pressed her ear against the door. She knocked and heard a soft moan as the loud TV played. Her heart lurched in her chest. Mabel was alive.

"Hang on, Mabel. Help is on the way."

****

Mabel lay unresponsive on the cart as the EMTs wheeled her down the porch from the elevator, then into the ambulance. Sif glanced at her phone. 12:40. The ambulance raced away with Mabel and Linda.

****

Sif paced from her living room to the entry. The sky glowed with pink and purple clouds as the sun rose. Her phone chimed, and she held it up. Linda.

"They did a triple bypass." Linda's voice was scratchy. Had she been crying? She must be drained.

"Will she be okay?" Sif clutched the phone.

"They said surgery went well. They've moved her to the ICU, but no one can see her until they move her to a regular room." She sniffed.

"You're exhausted. I'll be right there." Sif grabbed her keys and wallet and slipped into her coat. Mabel needed her and so did Linda.

****

Sif pulled the knotts out of the oven and set them aside to cool. She had been running on adrenaline for four days. She would crash, but when? She put another tray of knotts in the oven and set the timer. Martini rubbed against her leg.

"Let me take care of these cookies, then you get your snack." Martini meowed.

These stupid knotts. She should associate them with pain and heartache, and hate them, but she couldn't. Nanc made sure of that. She picked up the bowl of icing and stirred in orange zest, dipping her finger in for a taste. "Mm."

The tang of orange filled her mouth and scented the condo.

"Magic." Maybe she should make a wish? Nanc had christened them Christmas Wish Knotts, after all. She iced a cookie and nibbled the edge.

"I wish…"

No. Not that, not yet. She closed her eyes and tried again. "That Mabel makes a full recovery."

She sighed. Did Mabel have to eat one to make her wish come true? "Mabel, be strong. It's up to you now."

Sif dialed the hospital, staring out the picture window.

"Village Health Center," an operator said.

"Yes. I'd like to check on a patient, Mabel Sagan. She had heart surgery. Is she out of the ICU?"

"One moment, ma'am." The phone clicked, and she was on hold. Did that woman just call her ma'am? Nanc was right. She had become a *Quatre* Hen.

"Nurse Gillian here, you called about Mabel

31

Sagan?"

"Yes. I was wondering if she could have visitors today?" Sif glanced at the loons and gulls floating in the waves. Two sailboats tacked across the shipping lane.

"She can if you get here before two o'clock when she meets with the hospitalist and then has breathing and coughing exercises. If you can't, you might try after four o'clock."

"Oh, okay. Thanks." Sif disconnected. Was that nurse trying to keep visitors away?

The way the she'd drawled out "hospitalist" caught Sif's attention. The hospitalist could be Roger. Did Roger have a girlfriend at the hospital already?

Sif glanced at the clock on her stove, 12:45. If she left after this batch was out of the oven, she could get there and check out this Nurse Gillian.

She reached for a cookie tin and filled it with knotts for Mabel. Mr. Martini meowed.

"I know, buddy. We were supposed to grade papers and hang out today, but I have to check on Mabel." And Nurse Gillian.

The timer went off. She pulled out the knotts and put them on the cooling rack. Why did she even care about this nurse? Roger was nothing to her, right?

She donned her coat and checked her reflection in the mirror. Dark circles under her eyes again, but no time for cover-up. She grabbed the tin, ran her hand over Martini's back, and dashed out the door.

Would she run into Roger? Her stomach fluttered. Maybe her first wish would come true, too.

Chapter 5

Why Knott?

The elevator doors opened, and Sif glanced at the sheet of paper the lady at the information desk had handed her, "Room 418, fourth floor." A sign on the wall had an arrow pointing left for Rooms 400 to 420. She turned the corner and bumped into someone.

Startled, she put a hand on the wall to steady herself. "I am so sorry." She glanced up.

"Sif?"

"Roger?" She fumbled the tin, and Roger caught it.

"The one and only. It's a pleasure to run into you, but you have sharp elbows." He rubbed his ribs but smiled.

She chuckled.

"I wasn't watching where I was going. I'm looking for Room 418?"

He smiled, and Sif melted a little. He must workout, with firm muscles like…

"I need a break. Want to grab some coffee, see how the other half lives?"

"What?" She shook her head. "Of course. I've always…" Always what, Sif? Geez.

"The doctors' break room is just down the hall. It's a disaster, so brace yourself." He led her in the opposite direction of Mabel's room.

"Maybe a quick cup." She glanced at his slim hips.

Did they have beds in there? Her cheeks flamed. She didn't have to make this awkward, so why was she?

He hesitated. "Unless you're busy…"

"I came to visit Mabel—"

"Sagan? She's my patient, a real wonder woman. Triple bypass on Tuesday, and ready for pickleball on Wednesday."

"Really?"

"Well, no. I just really appreciate a patient who responds to treatment so well. Makes my job easier." He grinned at her.

She nodded, mesmerized by his self-confidence.

He leaned in. "You have the most amazing brown eyes."

"What?" She put a hand to her cheek. Where did that come from?

He leaned in closer.

She couldn't move. Her phone rang. She cleared her throat, pulling her phone out of her pocket. *That wasn't awkward at all.*

She glanced at her screen. Nanc. What timing. She held the phone to her chest. "Look, I have to take this, so maybe another time, okay?"

She rushed around a corner and answered.

"Nanc…" Sif leaned against the wall.

"A bunch of us are going out. Want to join us at the Village Public House?"

"Really? I don't know. Every time I go there…" Sif shook her head.

"You need to loosen up. Have some fun once in a while."

Sif glanced over her shoulder, but Roger was gone. She sighed. "I don't know. I guess—"

"Well, don't sound so excited. We're meeting at eight thirty for drinks. Music starts at nine."

Sif disconnected. Why did going out sound like work? She sighed. Would she ever get another invite to the doctors' break room? She slipped her phone in her pocket and, gripping her cookie tin, headed to Room 418, a hollowness in her chest.

Chapter 6

A Date

Sif pulled another student's paper from the stack on her dining room table. Sweet orange perfumed the air. Who was she kidding? She couldn't concentrate.

She dropped the paper and walked to the kitchen. She arranged a tin with cookies from the cooling rack. She could go for a run before the next rain shower, then she'd tackle her paper grading.

She glanced out the window, the lights of the pier twinkling off the rough waters of Puget Sound. She used to run with Biscuit in weather like this, but where was that dog now? With Boris and Shirley, of course. She missed stroking his silky ears.

She dried her eyes. Why did she always tear up? Because that dog loved her, and Boris—

Don't go there, Sif. She slipped on her shoes, tightening the laces.

Martini meowed. She dropped to her knees and drew him into her arms. "Who needs a slobbery, old dog, when I have you?" She set him on the floor in the hallway. He meowed and rushed to the door.

"I know you want to chase some birds, but no. Back, back, back." She put her hand down, and the cat raced into the living room as she slipped out the door.

She jogged down the steps and opened the back door to the parking lot. A car door opened, and she scanned the lot as Roger emerged from his Camry, his phone to his ear.

"I'll check his chart on my rounds in the morning. Yep. Good night." He slipped his phone into his pocket.

She walked down the side of the building. Maybe he hadn't seen her?

"We have to quit meeting like this."

She spun around and tried to act surprised. "We do live in the same building, so…"

He grinned at her. "Would you want to go out with me sometime?"

"Out?" She gasped and put a hand to her throat. *Get a grip. Say yes.* She ran her fingers over her hair. Wasn't she going to start brushing it?

"Well, yeah. On a date. Do you want to go? I mean—" He shrugged, and her heart melted. "It's fine if you don't…" He kept his eyes on his shoes.

Was she hurting him? That wasn't what she wanted, but she couldn't speak. Boris had used those same words the first time he'd asked her out. Was it a guy thing to ask, then backtrack in case the girl said no? She sighed.

"I didn't mean to…" He turned, and gravel crunched under his shoes as he walked away. "Have a good run."

"Wait." She swallowed and took a step toward him, holding up a hand. Her racing heart made her breathless, but she couldn't let him leave, not like this. She might not get another invitation from him. "It's not that I don't want to go on a date with you."

"So, does that mean you do want to go on a date?" He grinned, jingling his keys in his pocket.

"It's complicated." She shrugged. "I had a bad

breakup a while ago." *Really, Sif? A bad breakup?* It was a wedding nightmare, but she couldn't tell him that in the parking lot at eleven p.m.

"Why don't you come up for coffee sometime? I've been baking." She let the words hang in the air. His rumpled shirt and disheveled hair gave him a scruffy, end-of-the-day, ready-to-relax look that appealed to her.

He rocked on his heels, staring at a streetlamp. "Okay. Coffee and cookies? Start casual, I like it. When?"

He'd agreed, and he wasn't letting her off the hook. She hadn't planned this out very well. Now what? She scanned her brain. "Tomorrow's Saturday. Do you work?" She bit her bottom lip.

"It just so happens I don't. I've worked every day since I moved into Elgin's."

"You've worked fifteen days in a row? That's . . . a lot." Had she been keeping track of the days?

"Coffee and cookies sound great." He grinned. "What time?"

"Is nine thirty too early? I want to head to the hospital to see Mabel at eleven, and I can't be late or Nurse Gill…"

"Nurse Gillian?" He scoffed. "She can't tell visitors when to visit." Roger took her hand.

"She can't? But she did." There was something off about Nurse Gillian. She wasn't professional on the phone, and now Roger said she couldn't stop visitors? Sif frowned at her shoes. "How was I supposed to know?"

"I'll have a little chat with her on Monday. I'll see you at nine thirty." He turned, and whistling "Singing in the Rain," he trotted up the stairs.

She watched the ease with which he took the stairs. Nurse Gillian had better watch herself. She crossed the road, and a raindrop hit her on the nose. She chuckled. Who cared about a little rain? She put in her earbuds and called Nanc. "Guess who has a coffee date?"

"Do you know what time it is?" Nance yawned. "That's good because you were becoming a *Quatre* Hen before you were even thirty."

Sif scoffed. "Some best friend you are."

"The truth hurts, baby."

"Well, if it makes you feel any better, the *Quatre* Hens want me to move on too." Sif disconnected and raced down the pier, the raindrops falling faster.

Chapter 7

Neglected

Sif gazed at the Puget Sound, whitecaps rolling to the beach in the park. Roger would be here soon, and her stomach tightened in anticipation. Her phone rang.

"Mom? You got my message. Okay, but..." If she could get a word in, maybe they could have a conversation. "I left that message days ago." Sif hit speaker and placed the phone on the table.

"I'm sorry, honey, but the new sheep are taking all my time right now. They have lost weight and won't settle in, then there's the final construction on the sheep sheds, and our loan officers . . .. But enough of that. How are you?"

"I just wanted to see if you could make it to Christmas dinner. Do you think you can?"

"Maybe..."

Sif bristled at the pause. She wasn't coming. Again. Why was Mom putting her on hold like this? "Maybe? Come on, Mom. I might not be in this condo much longer."

"What? Why?"

"I'm a teacher, remember?" Sif couldn't imagine losing this place, and teaching an extra class helped pay the bills, but if the property taxes went up this year, she was screwed.

"Listen, the sheep are at a crucial phase in their

recovery. They were dehydrated and thin when they arrived, and I'm their person."

The view faded before Sif's eyes. "Their person?" How was this happening? She needed Mom, not this disappointment and rejection. It wasn't fair, but Dad always said, "There's no such thing as fair." He was right.

Her mom sighed into the phone. "You know they traveled all the way from Southern California. I need to monitor them twenty-four seven, and they need to produce milk by Christmas so we can show the bank we're meeting our benchmarks. The next couple of weeks are crucial for the business."

A twinge of guilt twisted Sif's stomach, but she pressed on. "So, you can't spare one day to celebrate Christmas? What about New Year's? Can't Jackie watch the sheep?"

"Listen, I'll know in the next week, okay? That's the best I can do."

"Mom…" Sif cradled the phone.

"Maybe you could come down here for Christmas. We could show you the new sheep sheds, and you could meet the new lambs. You'll fall in love."

Sif sighed. She could use some at-home time, but she'd already committed to helping Mabel with Christmas, and now she was in the hospital…

"I can't get away either. Just let me know."

"I will, honey. Bye."

"I love you."

Sif sank into the overstuffed chair. It held her like a warm embrace, and she pulled Martini into her lap.

"Sheep-shmeep. What about daughters, right, Martini?"

Martini pushed his nose against Sif's shoulder and purred. The doorbell rang.

"That must be the doctor, Martini. Just in time." She pushed herself from the chair ignoring the heaviness of the conversation with her mom. How could she put sheep above her own daughter?

She pulled the door open. Roger held out his hand.

"Flowers?" She grinned at him and took the bouquet.

"I was hoping you like them. Fresh flowers I mean."

She chuckled. "I love the spicy fragrance of carnations. Come on in."

Good call, Doctor. What woman didn't like fresh flowers? She opened the door wider so he could enter. He followed her into the kitchen as she pulled down a vase and put the flowers in water. She brought the bouquet to her nose and inhaled. He was thoughtful. But weren't they all at first?

"The water is hot, so I'll just get the French press started. Please sit." She motioned to the dining table and placed the flowers in the center.

Roger shuffled his feet, unsure what to do with his hands. He finally pushed them into his pockets. Was that why he was always jingling his keys? Nerves? Why would he be nervous around her? Sif poured water over the coffee and set the press on the table, by a plate of her orange Christmas Wish Knotts.

"It turns out I'm on call at ten o'clock this morning..." He shrugged his shoulders.

She did a double take. "Oh. So, you have to leave soon." So much for cookie wishes. "That's fine. We better talk fast." Was it fine, though? Tightness gripped her chest, and she forced a smile to her lips. First her mom's noncommittal response, and now Roger was cutting their coffee date short?

"Do you have time for one cup of coffee? Please have a cookie at least. I call them Christmas Wish Knotts. Do you like orange zest?" She was rambling. Why was she rambling? Her heart fluttered. *This was just coffee. Get a grip.*

"I'll make time." He grinned at her and sank into a chair, his eyes never leaving hers.

Maybe the Wish Knotts were working after all?

****

Sif stared at the clothes in her closet. What did one wear to a meeting with the dean? Business casual? She pulled out a black blazer and black pencil skirt. If she could sell her faculty development project, it would mean she wouldn't have to teach four classes in the spring quarter, so no extra papers to grade.

She laid the jacket out over the chair, running her fingers through her hair. If she didn't get this approval—

Think positive. Damn Boris, leaving her in the lurch.

She jumped at a knock on the door. Who could it be at this hour? She rushed to peek through the peephole. Roger? She tightened her robe belt and opened the door.

"Sorry," he said. "I know it's late, but I saw your light on, and I wanted to apologize again for this morning. I hated to cut our coffee date short." He jingled his keys in his pocket.

She reached out to place her hand on his arm but stopped as her robe belt slipped. She clasped the front of her robe.

"It's fine." She leaned against the doorframe, blocking the door. "What was the emergency?"

He stopped jangling the keys. "A patient had a bad reaction to a drug that needed to be sorted out. Did you do anything fun today?"

"Nanc came in the afternoon, and we went shopping."

"Nanc, is she the friend you were telling me about?" He ran his fingers through his hair.

"Yep." What did he really want? Would it be rude to ask? Very rude. She bit her lip and waited.

"I was wondering if you'd thought any more about going out with me? I mean for dinner or something? If you're busy that's—"

He was nervous. Did he feel obligated because he had to leave this morning? Maybe she should ask him if he'd be on call, like Mom and her sheep.

"No. I mean, yes—" She shivered but didn't want to invite him in and couldn't shut the door in his face. She tightened her grip on her robe.

"I found a great place right up in the Village. Wallace's. Know it?"

"Wallace's? Best chowder and Caesar salad in the Village." She smiled. He held her gaze and leaned forward. Was he going to kiss her? Her back stiffened, and he stepped back, but he was melting her again with his eyes again, and he seemed...what did he seem? Vulnerable? "When—?"

"Tonight."

"Tonight? What time is it?"

He pulled out his phone. "It's 12:16 a.m. So, yes, tonight." He grinned at her. "Your insomnia is working in my favor." He grinned.

She put a hand to her cheek. "I had no idea it was so late. I lost track of time again. I have an important meeting with the dean tomorrow. If all goes well, I won't have to teach an extra class this spring, so wish me luck."

"Good luck. I have a feeling you're going to nail it. You can tell me all about it at Wallace's." He stuffed his hands in his pockets and rocked on his heels. "So, it's a date?"

He was pretty cocky all of a sudden. Was this cookie magic again? She grinned. "It's a date."

He shook a finger at her. "But for now, I prescribe chamomile tea and bed this minute, so you're fresh for your meeting."

His shirt was open at the collar, and his tie hung from his coat pocket. She hadn't noticed the dimple in his chin before, but she sure did now. His hair was mussed, and a warm surge filled her, like being home. He exuded authority but was vulnerable at the same time. If he stood there much longer, she was afraid of what she'd do.

"Yes, sir, Doctor."

"I'll pick you up at six thirty tomorrow." He turned and disappeared down the porch.

She stared after him. The sway of his broad shoulders took her breath away. Chamomile tea? Please. She'd never fall asleep now.

****

Sif rushed out of the administration building and to her car. The meeting left her light and giddy. Clouds floated overhead in a blue sky, and chickadees chirped in the trees. A perfect day. Would it be a perfect

45

evening? She hopped in her car.

"Call Nanc," she said, and the car filled with ringing. Too many rings. She'd have to leave a message.

"I think I got the project, and guess who's going to Wallace's tonight." Sif squealed. "Call me."

She ended the call, and soft jazz filled the car. She hummed along, her stomach fluttering with each note. She drummed her fingers on the steering wheel, waiting for traffic turning into the park. This called for a run. She parked and grabbed her book bag. She slammed the car door and raced up the stairs to her condo.

She couldn't wait to hit the trail and burn off some of this excess energy. She'd run it in record time, then focus on her date with Roger. His grin, his white teeth, his ruffled hair, would he wear a tie? She glanced at her phone. 5:03.

She'd have to hurry. Should she wear the maroon dress or the moss green? She skidded to a stop. The Quatre Hens, sans Mabel, stood by the mailboxes.

"What?" She braced herself for an ambush.

Ellen had her hands on her hips, which was almost as daunting as Linda's arms crossed over her chest. Trudy grinned and shrugged her shoulders.

"What?" She couldn't wait to get out of these heels. Would have time for a run now?

"Christmas dinner will be here before we know it. Are you coming with your mom?" Ellen's chin dropped, and she frowned.

"I'll be there, but Mom still has to let me know. She's worried about the sheep, you know." Was Ellen nervous about filling Mabel's shoes? No one could, so she should relax.

"I need a head count." Ellen sniffed.

"I know, but she—"

"Are you bringing Boris or Roger?" Ellen took a step forward, and Sif backed against her car.

Boris? Why would she bring Boris?

"We like Doctor Roger Dodger." Trudy nodded.

Linda nudged Trudy. "You have to quit calling him that. If you say that to his face, how will you feel?"

Sif bit her lip. Since when did Trudy call him Doctor Roger Dodger? She chuckled, but why would they bring Boris up now?

"Will you? Ask Roger, I mean?" Trudy shifted from foot to foot, wringing her hands.

Sif put her heavy book bag on the floor and rubbed her shoulder. "Roger said he was coming, didn't he?"

"Yes, but ask him to come with *you*. It will make him feel more welcome." Trudy patted Sif's hand.

Did they know she had a date with Roger? Sif shook her head. "Okay. I'll ask him tonight. We're going to dinner."

Ellen nudged Linda, who nodded, and Trudy grinned.

"So, you are dating?" Linda's frown lines disappeared from her forehead. "We thought so."

"Roger and me? It's just dinner. We aren't—" Sif sighed and picked up her bag. Mabel would never have confronted her after work like this. The Quatre Hens needed Mabel to keep them from pushing their bossy old-lady noses in her business. Sif huffed.

Linda nodded at Ellen, and Trudy opened her mailbox. She sighed. Oh, so now she was being dismissed? In a daze, she climbed the stairs to the second floor, glancing over her shoulder at the entry.

They stood below her and waved. Sif lifted a hand in salute. What weren't they telling her?

Chapter 8

Food Coma

Roger opened the door to Elgin's condo, took her coat, and hung it on a hall tree. He led her to the love seat in the living room, and she curled against his side as waves nodded across the Puget Sound to Maury Island, and a fire glowed in the fireplace. She fit perfectly under his arm. Was this going to be a regular thing? She really wanted this to be a regular thing.

She closed her eyes. "Dinner at Wallace's wouldn't be complete without a food coma."

"Hmm." Roger's chest rumbled as he groaned, and Sif snuggled closer. "I had no idea Elgin's love seat was so comfortable. I was almost asleep."

He must be exhausted after putting in so many hours at the hospital. Still, he found the energy to be such a gentleman at dinner. The white tablecloths and halibut in butter sauce, the garlic risotto, and the sautéed green beans, not to mention the blackberry cobbler, and now sitting here in Elgin's condo, this was perfect. What she'd wished for. Her left arm tingled. Was it falling asleep? She didn't want to break the spell of cuddling with Roger as the view before them played like slow TV. Sailboats tacked in zigzags across the Sound, a cargo ship steamed through the middle channel, a couple of tugboats pulled a barge of gravel to Tacoma.

"This food coma might be permanent." Roger patted his stomach.

Sif laughed. Flames from the fireplace gave the room a golden glow, and Roger had opened the window a crack to let in salty air. She wanted his arm around her like this every evening. She glanced up at him. He was staring at her. A flutter of butterfly wings tickled her stomach as she made eye contact. She poked him in the side. "It's not nice to stare."

"I'm not staring. I'm admiring."

"Wow. Perfect comeback, but you're disturbing my food-coma Zen."

He chuckled and pulled her in close.

"Are you falling asleep?" She nudged him and he grunted. She sat forward, placing her feet on the floor.

He folded his hands behind his head and scrunched down. "I'm just getting comfortable. Who knows, I might want to buy my own condo in this beautiful building."

"Your own condo? Really?" He stiffened next to her. Had she ruined the moment? The last thing she wanted was to scare him away. *Keep it light, Sif.*

"I said might." He gave her a sideways glance that caught her off guard.

She sat on the edge of the love seat. "This sounds serious, Doctor. Perhaps we should consult on this."

"Perhaps we should." He grinned as he closed his eyes and pulled her against him. "I guess it all depends on Colorado."

Sif focused on the smallest sailboat. It bobbed, rather than glided, over the water. Was she that boat about to capsize? "Colorado?"

"It's my dream job. Don't hold it against me. I did

my internship there, and my plan was to go back after my residency. I'm done now, but I hadn't gotten to know Mabel, Elgin, the Quatre Hens…"

She pulled away.

"Or you." He reached for her, and she let him take her lips in a slow kiss that curled her toes. He released her, and she gazed up at him. "But it sounds like you still have trust issues since Boris. What if Boris comes back?"

Sif gazed out the window. Boris? He was the last thing she wanted right now. "If Boris comes back? I'll never fall for his lies again." She stopped. How much should she tell him? How much could he take? She glanced at him, but his eyes were closed.

"I find it hard to believe that you haven't dated since that—"

Sif broke in. "Hey. Dating was the last thing on my mind. I focused on teaching, baking, and friends. That was enough, until now."

Roger opened his eyes and sat up. "Until now?"

She stared into his dark eyes. "Yes. When a certain doctor came to town."

"Wait. You make me sound like Doc Holliday." He took her face in his hands, but she took his hands into her own.

"It's been rough. I'm not going to lie, but I learned a couple of things. The floor didn't open and swallow me, and even though being dumped broke me, I'm still standing." She glanced out the window. The little sailboat caught a wind, quit bobbing, and sailed straight into the marina. She grinned.

Roger tilted her chin up and brushed her cheek. "You are one strong cookie."

She snuggled into his side. "No cookie puns allowed."

Chapter 9

Roger Gets Plucked

A crisp wind blew through the length of the Cliff Edge Condos' porch, ruffling Roger's hair. He glanced at his phone. 9:48 a.m. Just enough time for a jog in the park before his shift. The Quatre Hens played cards at 10:00 a.m., though, so he'd have to hurry if he wanted to avoid them. He jogged down the stairs. If Mom hadn't called, he'd have been halfway through his run by now, but once she started with the questions, no one could stop her. Did Colorado call? Would he stay at the Village Health Center if Colorado didn't hire him? Were there any nice girls in the building? Of course, she'd want him to stay in Washington, close to her. If she weren't so clingy, he might want that too.

He scoffed. "Nice girls." Was she psychic? Someone might have told her about Sif. But who?

"Only a bunch of lovely old ladies, like you, Mom." He'd lied.

Sif. By the time Elgin had finished the introductions in the parking lot, he'd been smitten. He couldn't pay attention after that. She filled his mind when he should be concentrating on his patients. Was this growing into something serious? Maybe he should stay and find out, but…

Three months. That was the plan. Colorado would call and offer him the job, and he could begin his real career, at a real hospital, not some little hospital in the

Village. He'd been so sure about Colorado, but now? What was taking so long?

He closed his eyes. The sweet aroma of cookie dough followed that woman wherever she went, but how did she stay so fit? Must be the running, or she gave all the cookies away before she could eat them.

He grinned. Maybe he'd invite her out for a run sometime. He hit the landing and turned to jog down the final steps, but Linda stood at the bottom, glaring at him. Now what?

"Roger." Linda stood, arms crossed on her chest.

He sighed. She'd been waiting for him. He glanced at his watch.

"Do you have time for a quick cup of coffee and slice of Ellen's lemon cake?" She never made eye contact, but took in his hair, his shorts, his running shoes. What was this, an inspection? He was obviously going for a run.

"Lemon cake? But I'm—"

"Good. We're in the club room." She turned and marched away.

We? He followed. She led him through the door and he stopped. His heart sank. Ellen and Trudy sat waiting for him. He cleared his throat and glanced at Linda, then Trudy. "Is this about Mabel? She's improving every day." He reached for a piece of lemon cake. Who could resist it?

"Listen here, Doctor Roger Dod—" Trudy began.

Ellen placed a hand on Trudy's shoulder. Trudy clamped her mouth into a thin line. "So, Doctor Roger."

Roger glanced from Trudy to Ellen to Linda as they shifted in their seats. They seemed as uncomfortable as he was. "What can I do for you, ladies?" He sank into a chair.

"We are concerned about your intentions toward Sif." Trudy rolled her r's and glanced to Ellen and Linda, who nodded.

He coughed, the lemon bread dry in his throat. "Sif? Is she okay?"

"She's been hurt recently, and we can't let that happen to her again." Ellen folded her hands and placed them on the table in front of her, glaring at Roger.

"Hurt? You mean Boris?"

"She's too precious to us," Trudy said.

"She's like our granddaughter." Linda dabbed at her eyes with a tissue.

"Okay, but she's a grown woman, you know that, right?" Roger glanced from face to face. He wasn't sure what was going on here, and he glanced at his watch again. If he was going to get his run in before his next shift, he had to leave. Now.

"When she's nervous, all she does is bake cookies, and you know she's gluten intolerant, right?" Ellen glared at him. "She can't even eat them."

He shook his head. "So, she's gluten intolerant and—?"

"She's running a lot more, too, since you moved in." Linda glanced at the other Quatre Hens, who nodded.

"Since I—" So this was his fault? Didn't she want to spend time with him?

"You've upset her. Can't you see?" Ellen frowned.

"Wait, I've done what?" He squinted around the table. Had he misjudged Sif? Did she agree to go out with him just to be nice? The *Quatre* Hens sat like statues before him. *They're dead serious.* He adjusted himself in his chair and swallowed the last crumbs of dry lemon cake.

He cleared his throat. "Look. There must be a mistake. I wouldn't knowingly hurt—"

Linda shook her head. "We heard about the job in Colorado. You're not even sticking around."

"Don't play with our Sif. We have our eyes open to you." Trudy crossed her arms and harrumphed.

"That's 'eyes on you,' dear." Ellen patted Trudy's shoulder.

Linda stood. "Thanks for stopping by Roger. I think that's all for now."

What? Now he was being dismissed? He rose from the chair. First Mom, now the *Quatre* Hens, what had he done to deserve these interrogations? He pushed from the table and tipped his chair. He set it upright and rushed out of the room.

He paused on the sidewalk to tighten his shoelaces. Why were they so worried about Sif? He jogged across the street, lengthening his stride in the park. Was he coming on too strong?

His phone vibrated. He glanced at it. Nurse Gillian? What did she want? He needed this run more than ever, at least before he spoke with any more women. He silenced the ringer and sprinted through the park.

****

The *Quatre* Hens stood on the porch, gazing after Roger.

"Did he give us an answer?" Trudy asked. "He looks so upset."

"He's harmless." Ellen nodded to her friends. "But he'll behave himself now that he knows we're onto him." She put her hand on Linda's shoulder.

"He'd better," Linda said, and they filed back into the club room.

Chapter 10

Another Collision

Sif tied her running shoes, picked up Martini, planted a kiss on his forehead, and set him on the floor. He meowed and edged past her to the door.

"Back, back, back." She squeezed through the door. She grinned and jogged across the porch and down the stairs. What was this lightness filling her? She dashed across the street and into the park. The trees flew by as she pumped her arms. She glanced at her Fit-Time. 10:30. She needed to grade papers, but she couldn't sit still until she burned off some energy. She'd have to double-time it, and she put her head down and sprinted.

****

She moaned and shook her head. Someone was helping her sit, and his hands were warm and strong. She glanced through blurry vision.

Roger? Sweat beaded his forehead, and his elbow was bleeding.

"Did you fall?" She stood and the world spun.

"Fall? We both did, and it was more like a collision, though. You need to watch where you're going, Speed Racer." Roger frowned.

"What?"

He shook his head. "I guess I need to watch where I'm going, too. You blindsided me."

"I am so sorry." Heat rose to her cheeks. Had she run into him or he into her? She wobbled.

He gripped her hand. "Let's sit over here until you're steady." He led her to a bench. "Listen. About our date…" He stared out over Puget Sound.

She sighed. *Here it comes.* Was this about Colorado? He wasn't looking at her, so of course it was. Ice replaced the warmth flowing through her veins. He was leaving after all, but why bring it up here in the park? She peeked at his scraped elbow, then lowered her gaze. She was such a klutz sometimes. Was this thing between them over before it began? She wiped her nose on her sleeve.

"I know I've just met you, but you're the first real woman I've met in a while, and—" He shrugged, and she held her breath.

Real woman? Was he stuttering?

"What?" She sat stunned, waiting for him to go on, but he chuckled instead. Was he nervous? Because she sure was.

"But—" She glanced at him, and he took her shoulders in his large hands.

"No buts allowed." He pulled her to him.

She gasped, and he released her. She missed the warmth of him and shuddered. What was this about, and why didn't he kiss her?

She shook her head. "Listen, I'm sorry, but I—"

"No. I get it. I'm moving too fast. The *Quatre* Hens made that crystal clear." He jumped from the bench and jogged into the park.

Sif followed his form until he ran around a corner and disappeared into the forest. The *Quatre* Hens? She stood and stomped across the road to the condos.

****

Laughter rang through the club room door. Sif yanked it open, and silence met her as she charged into the room.

"What have you done?" She glared at the three women. They stared at the table or their cards. Trudy cleared her throat. Sif tapped her toe. "You must have said something."

"Whatever do you mean, dear?" Ellen batted her eyelashes.

Sif clenched her fists. "To Roger. What did you say to him?" Did they think she was stupid?

"We might have asked him a few questions." Trudy set her cards down in front of her.

"'Might' being the operative word here." Linda patted her blue-tinged hair.

Sif stomped her foot. "You ladies need Mabel more than you know. You don't think before you speak sometimes. Mabel would have stopped this before it got out of hand." She glanced out the window at the view.

Why did Mabel have to be in the hospital? She would have made them see reason, and Roger wouldn't—

Seagulls scolded each other over something on the beach. Their cries echoed through the air and the club room windows. They swirled over the shoal as the tide went out. Sif hung her head. Without Mabel, they would ruin everything before she and Roger even got started. Was it already too late?

"Won't you be our fourth today? You could fill in for Mabel." Linda motioned to Mabel's chair.

"We just want to see you happy before your thirty-sixth birthday." Trudy beamed at her.

"I am not thirty-six."

Linda kicked Trudy under the table.

Sif slumped into a chair and sighed. Happy? She was anything but happy.

"Only if you ladies tell me everything, from the beginning." But did she want to know the damage they'd done? Could she even fix it?

"Of course, Sif." They all nodded, and Ellen dealt the cards.

****

"What were you thinking?" Sif slammed a fist on the table, and the *Quatre* Hens jumped as one. She took a deep breath so her voice wouldn't shake. "You do not have to protect me. Okay? I'm not going to break. I'm just getting to know him."

"Did he tell you we only want to protect you?" Trudy turned pale, then pink, her hand rising to her lips.

Sif shook her head. Trudy kept her gaze on the green felt of the card table. "You know, Roger is the first guy I've even thought about since Boris, and this is what you do? Warn him about me?"

"We know." Trudy took off her glasses and rubbed the top of her nose. "*Mon dieu.* Mabel is going to boil our gizzards."

"I'm going to see Mabel today, and I'm going to tell her what you've done." Sif stood.

Linda popped from her chair. "No, no. No need for that. We'll tell her, dear, but what will you do about Roger?" Linda twisted a tissue in her hand, shredding it. "We didn't mean any harm."

"No harm? You say that now that you've scared him away?"

"We didn't do that, did we?" Ellen put a hand to

her face.

Sif rubbed her forehead. "You have no idea what you've done. I'll try to talk to him, if I can get close enough, because now he'll probably avoid me like the plague."

Sif stomped out of the room and ran up the three flights of stairs to her condo. She slipped inside and swept Mr. Martini into her arms. She glanced at the view and hugged the cat to her chest. He meowed.

"This is the first day I haven't thought of Boris. Not once." She buried her face against his neck, tears wetting his fur.

Chapter 11

A Surprise Visit with Mabel

Sif pulled into the Village Health Center parking lot and lifted her tin of cookies from the passenger seat. Mabel loved her knotts, no matter the flavor or what she called them—Friendship, Good Luck, Christmas Wish. She pulled out a cookie and bit into it. She was beyond caring about gluten. Would Mabel be able to help her? She brushed the crumbs off and climbed out of the car. Would she run into Roger? She shut her car door and locked it.

She adjusted the tin under one arm and her bag on the other, then froze. Roger was racing across the parking lot right toward her. She glanced behind her, then at the four-story hospital. Was he headed for her?

No. His dark eyes blazed, and his hair blew as he charged to her. She opened her mouth to ask him what was wrong, but he reached her, took the tin of cookies, placed it on the roof of her car, then pulled her into his arms. What was he—

He pressed his lips to hers, and she melted. He held her against him as his mouth crushed her lips, and she fell into him, wrapping her arms around him. He released her lips, and she stumbled. She was panting, and he held her shoulders to steady her.

He gazed into her eyes. "I've wanted to do that since this morning when you bulldozed into me."

She lifted a finger to her lips and gazed at him. "You wanted to kiss me, but?" She took a step back and wobbled. He'd annihilated her with one kiss. "Why didn't you?"

Her pulse pounded through her veins as she stood in his embrace. She wanted him to kiss her again and never stop. She leaned against him, absorbing his warmth. He had wanted to kiss her since this morning. How had she missed that vibe?

"I wanted to, but the *Quatre* Hens kind of warned me off." He lowered his eyes to hers and caressed her hands. "They are a force." He chuckled.

Was he blushing? She shook her head. "The *Quatre* Hens mean well, but—"

"They told me about, you know..." A breeze blew his white jacket open and set his Mickey Mouse tie flapping. "I just want to get to know you better."

She squeezed his hand. "I want that too." She gazed into his eyes. Were they smoldering? She wanted to take him in her arms and smother him with another kiss but sighed instead. Way to go, cookie magic.

Her heart pounded as they walked toward the hospital arm in arm. Could she forgive the *Quatre* Hens? Of course she could, and maybe she should thank them because now she didn't have to tell him about—

Don't ruin the moment, Sif.

She walked in a daze by his side. The windows reflected the blue sky. Which window was Mabel's? She caught a movement. Was that Nurse Gillian frowning right at her? Or was she frowning at Roger? Whoever it was backed into the darkness. Had Sif imagined her there? She shivered.

"You're cold. We'd better get you inside quick." He smiled down at her.

It wasn't the cold, but she didn't correct him. "Oh, I forgot my cookies. They're on the roof of my car." She couldn't visit Mabel empty-handed, but she didn't want to let go of Roger's hand either.

"No worries." Roger jogged to her car and returned handing her the tin of cookies.

They walked through the hospital lobby shoulder to shoulder, his warmth a reminder of his kiss. They reached the elevators way too soon for Sif. He stopped and grinned. Was he going to kiss her again?

"Can I see you tonight?"

She ran her tongue over her lips, the minty taste of him still there. "What time?"

Two date nights in a row? All she had to do was talk to Mabel so she could keep the *Quatre* Hens from interfering anymore.

"Around seven. Let's say dinner at the Edge of the Sea?" He was backing away.

She nodded. Of course, he had to go. She hugged the cookie tin. "Sounds perfect."

"Meet me in the lobby at seven?" He lifted his hand in farewell. "Maybe I'll see you in Mabel's room." He grinned and walked away.

She lifted a hand in a small wave and stepped into the elevator. It stopped at each floor to let people off as she replayed the kiss over and over. Would things be awkward between them the next time they met? Of course not. They'd kissed before, but today's kiss…

She breezed out of the elevator. Voices came from Room 418, and one of them had a French accent. How had the *Quatre* Hens beat her here? She lifted her hand to knock, and Linda's voice said, "Then Trudy told him about the WD."

They told Roger about the wedding debacle? Oh man, they didn't spare any of the details. She had already hinted at it, but geez. Besides, he had just met her in the parking lot and kissed her like . . .

She scoffed. There was nothing to worry about. She smiled, still filled with the warmth of Roger's lips on hers.

Trudy's voice rose. "You are telling on me? What about you?"

"Settle down. The damage is done. It's up to them now." Mabel's voice came out like molasses over gravel, thick but raspy.

It *was* up to her and Roger, and the kiss in the parking lot was a step in the right direction. Her stomach filled with flutters. She couldn't wait for tonight and her dinner with him. She knocked on the door.

"Well, look who comes bearing gifts. Our very own Norse goddess." Mabel grinned from her hospital bed, tubes running from her arm to a pole by the bed. She sat like a queen bee in charge of the hive that buzzed around her. "Ellen, be a dear. There's a spare chair in the hall."

Sif smiled as she lifted the lid and presented the tin of cookies topped with a bow. Mabel laughed, never taking her eyes from the tin filled with butterscotch balls as she accepted them. She was on the mend, and the twinkle in her eye calmed Sif. What would she do without Mabel?

A knock on the door, and Roger walked in with Nurse Gillian tagging on his heels. She was giggling at something, and he had a stupid grin on his face. This was Mabel's nurse, and she worked on the same floor as Roger? Her uniform was cinched tight around her tiny waist, and Sif wanted to gag.

They were here to take care of Mabel, but they acted like they were off duty. Did he also want to get to know Nurse Gillian better? It seemed like she wanted to get to know him. The room spun, and she lifted her fingers to her lips.

Nurse Gillian batted her eyelashes at Roger as she took the tin from Mabel. "I'll take those. I could smell the butter from the hallway." She didn't even glance at Mabel. "You shouldn't have these. I'll just put them in the break room."

"Hmm?" Roger hadn't lifted his gaze from Mabel's chart.

He wasn't even paying attention to her. Ha. Take that, missy. Sif crossed her arms. Nurse Gillian frowned as Roger made notes on the page.

He glanced up. "What did you say?"

"The cookies. Surely Mrs. Sagan can't have these after her—"

"Of course she can." Roger took the cookie tin and handed it back to Mabel. "Quit telling people what they can and can't do before you check with me."

Nurse Gillian frowned and grabbed a bag of saline solution.

Mabel batted her eyelashes. "Thank you, Doctor."

Was Mabel flirting? Sif shook her head, and Trudy giggled, while Linda patted her hair. Ellen sat with her mouth hanging open. All female eyes were on Roger, and he'd only glanced up from the chart once to give Mabel the cookies back. Was he that oblivious to all this estrogen?

He signed the chart and smiled at Mabel. "You can have *one*, the rest you share." Roger handed the chart to Nurse Gillian. "Good news. You can go home on Monday if your vitals remain stable." He smiled and placed his hand on Mabel's shoulder, then turned to Sif and whispered, "Can I see you in the hallway?"

"But Doctor, the—" Nurse Gillian stuttered but couldn't distract Roger.

"Check her IV, Nurse," he said and gave a slight bow to the *Quatre* Hens. "Keep up the good work, ladies. These visits are the best medicine for my star patient."

Mabel simpered in her pillows. Trudy, Ellen, and Linda watched as Roger took her hand. Sif tried to keep the grin from her lips but failed. She caught Nurse Gillian's glare as she swapped the solution bag on Mabel's IV pole.

"See you soon, Mabel. Bye, ladies." Sif waved, and Roger led her down the hall and around a corner.

"What did you—" Sif looked up.

Roger leaned forward, and taking her chin in his hand, he covered her lips with his. She couldn't move, couldn't breathe, but his tongue flicked against her teeth, and she opened her mouth. He pressed her against the wall as he explored her lips, and she clung to him.

He pulled away and gazed into her eyes. She had to tilt her head back to keep eye contact, her lips tingling.

"I'm sorry. I can't help—"

"Don't be sorry. I'm not." She was grinning like a fool, but she didn't care. She wanted more, more lips, more tongue, more pressing. Kissing was like riding a bike, you never forgot how. He grinned at her, and her pulse rose as he held her hands.

"I can't be in the same room with you and not want to do that."

Sif licked her lips. "Well, that is an interesting problem, Doctor." Flirting was like riding a bike, too. "When did these symptoms first appear?"

He chuckled and tightened his grip on her hands. "One night by the mailboxes when someone couldn't sleep, but I had to rush to the hospital." He kissed her again.

She thrilled at his touch and leaned into him, spicy cologne filling her senses. She closed her eyes and put a hand on his warm, firm chest. "So, what's the prognosis?"

"Prognosis? I think dinner tonight to begin with." He chuckled.

She reeled. Two kisses and a date, could today get any better? She had a lot to get done if she was going to enjoy tonight guilt-free. "I better go finish grading papers. I'll see you at seven."

He released her hands shoving his in his pockets. "Until then."

Her stomach fluttered. Butterflies? The butterflies were back. After that last kiss, she might become a butterfly.

He pecked her on the cheek, grinned, and headed down the hall, jingling his keys.

Sif floated to the elevators and stepped through one with open doors, hit the button, and leaned against the wall. What would she wear, and where did he learn to kiss like that?

She hugged herself. She had a date. Was she moving on, or what? She couldn't wait to call Nanc.

She sighed as the elevator rumbled to the lobby.

Chapter 12

Moving On

Sif unlocked her door and poked her foot inside to stop Martini from rushing out. Dinner with Roger. Her tummy fluttered. Should she wear the red dress with the little black jacket and low heels, or her LBD with the maroon jacket and stilettos? Mr. Martini rubbed against her ankle, and she scooped him up and buried her face in his fur.

"Oh, Martini, I have another date. Can you believe it?" She put the cat down. She hadn't gotten this excited about anyone since the wedding and Boris...

Roger was nothing like Boris.

She sighed and sank into a chair by the picture window. Boris had been so funny and sweet in college. Was it really six years ago? After a football game at the victory rally, an aura of spice hung around him, pulling her in. They'd talked for hours, and her stomach hurt from laughing so hard. He'd had the confidence to redshirt, and even though he didn't play much, his eyes shone as he talked about practice and his teammates.

"I get the best seat in the stadium for every game," he'd said. It was that positive energy that attracted her. She wanted that for herself. She shook her head. But Shirley had won that prize. What if—

Stop it. That chapter was over, and she had a date with Roger. Mmm.

Whitecaps frothed on the Sound, and dozens of sailboats careened across the water. She ran her fingers through Martini's fur. She got the condo after Boris had jilted her, but the part that hurt the most was the loneliness. She was supposed to be with someone, but not him.

"You have to let go of the past," her mom had said, and she was right, but that was an easy thing to say.

She opened the window, and a salty breeze blew in. She let it fill her lungs, clear her head. She picked up her phone and called Nanc, hit speaker, and placed the phone on the coffee table.

"Hey, girl." Nanc was in a good mood today.

Sif grinned. "Hey. You busy?"

"Just finishing this deposition, then I'm out of here. What's up?"

"Roger kissed me."

"What? Where?"

"On the lips." Sif pulled a pillow to her chest and curled up on the couch.

Nanc scoffed. "You know what I mean. Details. Tell me."

"It was in the hospital parking lot this morning, and I can't even describe how wonderful it was." Sif sighed.

"It's a sign, and you should follow it." Nanc was practically shouting. "So, when do I get to meet this Doctor Roger? Is he cute?"

"He is. He's the hottest guy in the building." Sif set the pillow aside and let Martini climb on her lap.

"Ha-ha. He doesn't have to try very hard." Nanc scoffed. "But really, I'm so happy for you. Now you can forget about Boris once and for all. Move on to greener pastures. Let's see, what other old cliches can I dig up?"

Sif chuckled. "Okay, I get it. I've got to get ready. I'm seeing him tonight." She set Martini on the floor and stretched.

"Well, go forth and be of good cheer, milady, win the heart of prince charming, and all that other Shakespeare stuff."

"Leave Shakespeare out of this, thank you very much." Sif picked up her phone and took it off speaker. "Thanks, Nanc."

"I want a full report."

"You'll be the first person I call." Sif ended the call. What would she do without Nanc? "Now what to wear on my date." She hummed "Jingle Bells" as she wandered into her closet and pulled out the red dress. She held it in front of her as she turned from side to side in front of the mirror. "Perfect."

****

The maître d' pulled out a chair for Sif, and she tripped over the leg. Roger was accepting menus from the waiter. Had he noticed how clumsy she was? She sat and pretended not to be embarrassed. He passed her a menu.

"Any recommendations?" Roger glanced up at the waiter.

The waiter leaned over Roger's shoulder and pointed to an item on the menu. He whispered in Roger's ear, and Roger pulled away. The waiter grinned and sauntered to the kitchen.

"What did he say?" Sif spread her napkin on her lap.

"He said anything on the menu was good, and he liked my belt buckle." Roger's cheeks grew pink.

Sif put a hand to her mouth to hide her smile. Even men found him attractive. "Your belt buckle? How did I miss the belt buckle? Stand up." Sif waited as Roger shook his head.

"No. I'll just tell you. It's my grandpa's championship rodeo buckle from the Omak Stampede in 1968." He turned even more crimson.

"How could I miss the rodeo champ buckle from 1968? Now you have to show me." She stood.

Roger waved his hands for her to sit. "All right, all right." He stood and put his thumbs behind the buckle and tilted it back and forth. The sterling silver buckle glittered under the chandeliers, and Sif made out a silver dollar in the ornate buckle.

"Oh. Very classy. Is this your 'first-date' buckle?" She used air quotes and grinned at him. She'd missed laughter. "I think he was admiring more than your buckle." She raised her eyebrows at him, and he gave her a glare. Too far? She clamped her mouth shut.

The waiter came back with two waters and a basket of bread and garlic butter. The Edge of the Sea was famous for their artisan sourdough bread. Sif's mouth watered. She'd taken her gluten pill, and she couldn't wait for a warm slice of melted butter perfection.

"Can I start you off with any beverages?" The waiter winked at Sif, and she grinned.

Yes, he's with me.

"I was thinking a Riesling, but what do you think? Shall we share a bottle?" Roger smiled.

Heat rose from her chest to her cheeks. Stupid, stupid, stupid. How could she forget to tell him she didn't drink?

"I'd actually like a soda water with a slice of lime.

I teach a final tomorrow at eight a.m." She nodded to the waiter and adjusted in her seat, unable to meet Roger's eyes. Alcoholism, it was right up there with gluten intolerance, kind of gross and very personal.

"Oh, okay. Gin and tonic on the rocks for me, then."

The waiter smiled at Roger, spun on his heel, and sped to the bar.

"Sorry about the Riesling."

"No, don't be."

"So, do you ever drink?" He'd lost his smile, and she missed it.

"No. I'm sorry I didn't tell you before. We have a lot to learn about each other."

"Now I know." He reached across the table and took her hand.

"I'm so sorry I teased you about the belt buckle." She giggled.

"Me too." He scowled at her, then grinned. "It's never gotten that kind of attention before." He shrugged. "When did you quit?"

"I haven't had a drink since I graduated from college five years ago. My favorite uncle died in a car accident. He was an alcoholic."

Roger took her hands in his. Sif sighed as they wove their fingers together. She could sit like this holding hands forever. He never passed judgement, even when she was telling him her darkest secrets. Maybe she could pull this off without blowing it after all. He winked, and she glowed in the warmth of his smile.

"So, what's the catch of the day?"

"I hope you like lobster." He stared into her eyes.

Lobster? That's what she had on her first date with Boris.

Don't go there, Sif.

She shook her head and gazed across the room at their waiter, who leaned into another male customer, then she squeezed Roger's hands. "Sounds delicious."

Chapter 13

The Day After

Grading Shakespeare explication papers at the end of the quarter made Sif want to wash all her windows or visit her dentist or—bake a batch of cookies.

How could she concentrate when her thoughts kept rehashing dinner at the Edge of the Sea? She wrote a final comment at the end of a paper and paged through to tally her marks. She filled in the grading sheet, starting with the strengths, then pointing out the weaknesses. She added a smiley face at the end.

One of her classes had counted all the smiley faces she'd put on everyone's papers and came up with a class total of 562 by the end of the quarter. She took that as a compliment.

Five papers done. Time for a break. She picked up her phone and called Mom. It rang and rang. She must be in the barn again. She lived out there these days.

"Hello?" crackled over the line, startling her.

"Mom? How's it—"

"Hi, honey. I'm in the barn. We have the vet here, so—"

"I figured, but Christmas is coming, and the *Quatre* Hens are pre—" Sif held the phone to her ear.

"I'm sorry, honey. We have a problem with Betty Boop. She's our leader-sheep from Iceland, and the vet can't figure out what's wrong. We can't lose—"

She held out the phone and glared at it. "Okay, Mom, but isn't Betty Boop pregnant? Maybe she's just in labor?" She tapped her foot.

"She is pregnant, but it's five weeks too early." Mom's voice echoed as she walked through the barn.

Sif scratched her head. "Mom, I know you're busy, but Ellen needs an answer. Please say yes."

"Honey, I won't make promises I can't keep. If Betty gets an all clear from the vet, I should be able to make it, but I just won't know until he's run all the tests."

She nodded. "Keep in mind that Ellen is not Mabel, who could organize a feast for Queen Elizabeth II. Maybe I should just say you're coming, and then you can let me know for sure."

"I like that plan. By the way, how's Mabel?"

"Mabel is coming home Monday. She has a wonderful doctor who—"

"Doctor? Not the doctor that moved into your building. I hear he's single. You should make your mo…"

Sif frowned. "Okay, bye, Mom."

She sank into the cushions of the chair, and Martini hopped in her lap. She held him to her chest. "Matchmaking mothers. Am I right, Martini?" She rubbed her nose into his fur, then set him on the floor and picked up another paper to grade. Her phone rang. Now what? She dropped the paper.

"Hello?"

"Sif, is that you?"

"Linda?"

"It's Elgin. He's back in the hospital." Linda's voice faltered

"What?" She fumbled the phone. "When?"

"Just now? The knee surgery went so well, and he was doing great, but apparently, he had a reaction to the pain meds. I have to make six more calls." The line went dead.

Sif dropped the phone on the counter.

Elgin was back in the hospital? She filled Martini's kibble dish and washed her hands, then set about filling a cookie tin with knotts and butterscotch balls. She bit into a knott and wished for Elgin's recovery. She cleared the counter, then ran a washcloth over it. A recipe card in her grandmother's beautiful script sat on the counter, discolored, and stained. signs of love. The smell of butterscotch and orange brought visions of Christmases at Nana's, decorating the tree, sipping hot chocolate, sneaking down to catch Santa putting presents under the tree.

Elgin needed that kind of joy. She focused on her wish for his recovery as she tucked the recipe card back into her *Cookies* cookbook. She paused to glance out the window. Several small boats sailed across Puget Sound, their colorful sails like flowers on the water. She grabbed her car keys and cookie tin and headed out the door. Student papers would have to wait.

****

Sif rushed into the hospital clutching her tin of cookies. She srode up to a woman behind the information desk and reading her name tag said, "Hello, Estelle."

The woman glanced up and smiled. "May I help you?"

Roger rounded the corner, and she juggled the cookie time almost dropping it as he approached. She bit her lip.

"Sif." He grinned.

Her stomach fluttered at the sound of her name. It left her craving his lips on hers. Would he kiss her again, right here?

Roger glanced at his watch. "Is school out already?"

"It's study day, and my schedule is crazy, but how did you know?"

"I'm observant."

She smiled and let the warmth of his eyes envelop her. "I came as soon as I heard about Elgin."

He nodded, then crossed his arms over his chest. "Elgin could do with a pretty visitor, especially one bearing cookies. Which leads me to ask, Professor, did Shakespeare eat cookies or not? Inquiring minds want to know."

She grinned. He'd remembered her story from last night about the Shakespeare Knotts. "Of course he did, and the knotts were a big hit in class, by the way." Her stomach flipped as his laughter filled the hall. "But more importantly, inquiring minds want to know how Elgin is doing."

His smile disappeared, and he took her elbow. Her throat seemed to close.

"He called me a quack and fired me." He stared at her with a straight face.

Sif pulled her arm away and pushed his shoulder. Roger laughed, and the flutters in her stomach rose to her chest. "You are a quack." She gazed into his eyes. "He's lucky to have you, you know."

She'd backed out of the middle of the hallway and against the wall to allow a nurse pushing a wheelchair to pass, and Roger leaned in closer.

"The *Quatre* Hens think you preformed a miracle on Mabel." She tried to keep the shaking out of her voice.

"Ellen told me when she officially invited me to the Cliff Edge Condo Christmas Dinner." He chuckled, and she wanted to grab him and pull his lips to hers.

"Will Elgin be able to make it, too?"

"I'll make sure he's out of the hospital in time for Christmas," he said, the wrinkles at the corners of his eyes deepening the rich shadows in his dark eyes. "Do I have to worry about Elgin? You are all he talks about."

"Me?" He was leaning closer. Was this where he kissed her? She could smell his minty breath, just like last night. The flutter in her chest turned to a jackhammer, and she parted her lips.

"There you are, Doctor." Nurse Gillian sashayed up to Roger. "We're waiting for you to check Mrs. Graham's charts."

Nurse Gillian? How rude. Sif wanted to grab her by the hair, but she clenched her fists instead. Of course, Roger was busy, but Sif wanted her kiss.

"Right. I'm coming." He didn't take his eyes from Sif as he spoke, and she held his gaze. Take that, Nurse Gillian. "Excuse me, but duty calls. See you later." He turned and was gone.

The cookies rattled in the cookie tin as Sif clutched it, trying to slow her heart rate. She turned to the information desk.

Estelle smiled. "Who were you looking for?"

Sif smiled and adjusted her cookie tin. "Elgin Gluckmeister, please."

Estelle ran her finger down the screen. "Third

floor. Check with the nurse's station. They can direct you."

"Thanks." Sif rode the elevator to the third floor, but Roger filled her mind, his dark eyes, his lips on hers, his hands—

The doors opened, and the cookies shifted in the tin as she stepped into the hallway, the elevator doors closing behind her. She stepped into a lobby, couches arranged in an alcove, a TV blaring with the local weather report. A plaque on the wall read Birthing Center. They put Elgin with the new moms? He must be in heaven. She chuckled.

She rounded the corner but lurched to a stop. Nurse Gillian smiled up at Roger and standing on her tiptoes adjusted his collar. Did she just kiss his lips? Sif staggered. Roger grinned at something Gillian said, and the floor seemed to fall away. She leaned against the wall. They hadn't spotted her yet, so she spun around, ducking around a corner. Was this Shirley and Boris all over again?

She clutched her stomach. Why had Roger kissed her? He'd been professional with Gillian in Mabel's room, but this wasn't professional at all. Yet Boris hadn't seemed interested in Shirley, either. Or had he? Her mind spun with images of Boris during those meetings. Shirley giggling and him pouring her coffee. How had she not seen the signs? Well, she wouldn't repeat that mistake. She couldn't afford to.

She glanced down the hall and gasped. Nurse Gillian hugged Roger. Her hand rose to her throat. She shook her head, unsure of what was happening. They were frickin' hugging. That was what was happening, but why? He rocked her from side to side, and Sif couldn't tear her gaze from their long embrace. They seemed comfortable together. Had they hugged like this before? Had they kissed too? Her lip began to quiver. She'd believed him when he said he cared. What a liar.

No, she wouldn't be made a fool of again, not like Boris. An exit sign glowed at the opposite end of the hall from Roger and…

She dropped the cookie tin as she ran to the door. It opened to a stairwell, and she glanced back at Roger. He smiled down at Nurse Gillian, and Sif raced down the stairs. He hadn't even noticed her. She sobbed as she ran.

Her mind raced through scenes of her wedding day. All eyes had been on her as she held her bouquet. Her stomach cramped as she reached her car, yanked the door open, and plopped in the front seat with a sob.

She'd just met Roger. What did she really know about him? Nothing, obviously. The image of him rocking Gillian from side to side in his warm embrace, smiling down at her face. She pounded the steering wheel.

"Get a grip." She put the key in the ignition but stopped. She was forgetting something. "Oh, no," she moaned. Oh no, the cookie tin. She'd dropped it when she bolted. What a disaster. She had to go back and get it, but what if Roger and Gillian were still…

She rubbed her face with her hands. This was what she got for letting her guard down. What made her think she was ready to date? But his eyes, his smile…

Don't be ridiculous, Sif.

They'd shared a couple of romantic dinners, some pretty great kisses, but that was all. It meant nothing to him. She sank into her seat and stared at the steering wheel. Should she confront him? Should she go back for her cookies and visit with Elgin, as though her world wasn't falling apart?

No. She'd go home and put on her fuzzy pajamas and grade papers. She pinched the skin at the bridge of her nose to stop the headache. The steering wheel blurred as her tears fell.

A tap on her car window startled her, and she dabbed at her eyes. Linda and Trudy stood holding her tin of cookies. Would they know she'd been crying?

She opened the car door. "Hi." She stared at the tin, but all she saw was Nurse Gillian kissing Roger and Roger kissing her back. She sighed, unable to look at her friends.

"We saw you drop these in the hall." Linda handed her the tin. "Are you all right? You look like you've seen a ghost."

"*Oui, un fantôme.*" Trudy wrung her hands and nodded.

"Didn't you want to bring these to Elgin? He's waiting for you." Linda held out the tin.

They knew what she'd seen, and they weren't going to let her wallow in her tears. This was gruff Linda, the Brunhilda of the group. Linda always surprised her by caring when Sif least expected it.

She sighed and swung her legs from the car. They were so heavy, and the last thing she wanted was to trudge back in the hospital. What was she afraid of, though? She didn't do anything wrong. She'd show Roger. He could have his nurse, and she'd keep her sanity, thank you very much.

Linda reached for her arm, and she nodded. "Let's go."

Trudy clasped her hand. "He's in Room 326."

Sif squeezed Trudy's hand, and Linda carried the tin.

"Where's Ellen?" Sif searched the parking lot.

"She's babysitting the brats. I mean her granddaughters." Linda snorted.

Sif chuckled. Ellen's granddaughters were little angels, and Ellen adored them. Linda's humor was a much-needed distraction. Sif filled her lungs and exhaled slowly as she strolled through the lobby. She'd hold her head high and ignore Roger and Nurse Gillian.

Trudy nodded to Estelle. Sif wanted to melt into the floor, but she met Estelle's eyes. The woman nodded. She rode the elevator in silence, sandwiched between her friends, and she tightened her grip on Trudy's hand. The doors opened, and Linda and Trudy bustled around the corner to Elgin's room. Sif hung back. What would she do if Nurse Gillian or Rog—

"Sif?"

Sif spun around. Roger stood, hands on hips, grinning at her. "Did you take the scenic route? I expected you twenty minutes ago."

"What?" He had a lot of nerve. She couldn't meet his eyes. "Elgin's waiting for me, then I have to get home and finish grading." Why was he acting like he hadn't kissed Nurse Gillian? Did he think he could have them both?

He reached for her hand, and a familiar tingle raced up her arm. She ignored it.

He twined his fingers with hers. "I have to check his chart, but I must warn you. He's feeling much better, so you might need protection."

If his hand wasn't so warm and his eyes so soft,

she might be able to pull her hand away. Was this when Nurse Gillian arrived? Her timing was impeccable. He led her into Elgin's room. Trudy and Linda stood by the bed, and Linda handed her the tin.

"There you are. These two wouldn't give me the cookies until you got here." Elgin raised a limp hand to Sif. "Said I needed doctor's approval."

"Your doctor has the final word," Linda said, and Trudy nodded.

Sif forced a smile and glanced at Roger. Why was Elgin so weak? The effort it took for him to lift his hand. Her stomach tied in a knot. She glanced at Roger again, but he didn't seem concerned. Elgin grinned at her, and she leaned down and kissed his cheek. He held out his palm like a beggar and cocked his eyebrow at her.

Roger chuckled, and Sif thrilled at the sound. He took Elgin's hand and placed it on the bed. "No cookies for you, mister, not until you can keep down something besides orange gelatin."

"You're no fun." Elgin rolled his head on the pillow, unable to lift it.

Roger read Elgin's blood pressure and recorded it on his chart.

"So, am I going to live?"

Sif put a hand to her chest. Would Elgin be recovered in time for Christmas? And even if he would, would they ever run together again? She glared at Roger. Was he keeping something from her? "Elgin. Don't—"

Elgin seemed in worse shape than the day after surgery. But Linda and Trudy didn't seem to be worried either. Was it just her?

"I'm seventy-eight, you know. It's not like I'm going to rebound like some young dude, like the doc here, but I'm on the mend." Elgin grinned and sank into the pillow.

"That's the spirit." Roger grinned at Elgin and winked at Sif.

She shook her head. What was wrong with these two? She sniffed. Nurse Gillian would probably be able to handle this, no problem, but she was falling apart. All she could offer were cookies and hugs. She dabbed at her eyes and wiped her nose.

"I'm so sorry this happened, Elgin." She took his limp, cool hand and squeezed it. Maybe she could offer him a drink? Wipe his brow?

Elgin lay back and closed his eyes, exhausted.

Roger put a hand on Elgin's shoulder and smiled. "I hate to cut this visit short, ladies, but I think nap time is in order for this young man."

"Kill joy." Elgin swatted the air, but he didn't open his eyes.

"We have to pick up Ellen anyway," Trudy said.

"More like save her from those granddaughters." Linda jiggled her car keys and grinned. She put her arm in Trudy's, and the two ladies departed.

Sif released Elgin's hand. "Me too. I mean, I have papers to grade."

Elgin nodded, and she took a step back. Cookies were the last thing he needed right now. Roger took her by the elbow and steered her from the room and into the hall. He walked her around a corner as tears streamed down her face.

"You said Elgin was fine." She jerked away from him.

"He's doing as well as can be expected."

"Then why was he so weak?" She sobbed, and Roger rubbed her shoulder, oblivious to her anger. She flinched away. "He's never been so weak. Are you sure he's okay?"

"He's had an adverse reaction to his pain meds, but we've changed them, and he's responding well. His heart and pulse are strong, and he's not in any danger. All he needs is hydration and sleep, and he'll be his old self again. He'll probably go home tomorrow afternoon."

"Really?"

"Really. Dehydration is his worst enemy right now, so he's in the right place."

"Well—" She dabbed at her eyes.

"He'll be fine, I promise." Roger took her by the shoulders. "You seem angry about something. What's up?"

This was her chance to ask about Nurse Gillian. The words stuck in her throat. "I better let you get back to your rounds," she mumbled, and stuffing the tissue into her pocket, she rushed away.

She sat in her car and stared at the yellow stripe on the garage pillar. Would Elgin be able to walk, let alone run again? Her lips quivered. Why did the people she love always leave her? Had she lost Roger before she even had him? Was he already moving on to Nurse Gillian? She sighed. Well, if that were the case, they deserved each other.

She sniffed, blinking back the tears as she started her car and drove from the parking lot.

Chapter 14

Loneliness

Sif swung her legs out of bed and stretched to the ceiling. Her sprint through the park had left her stiff, and she smiled as her back popped. Dirty clothes lay scattered across the bedroom floor.

Coffee.

She picked up clothes on her way to the kitchen and threw them in the utility room. Her stomach growled.

Breakfast.

What did Roger like for breakfast? Maybe she should call him, invite him up for waffles? He hadn't given her his number, but she hadn't given hers either. They saw each other every day, so why bother? But still...

She buzzed through the condo, dusting, collecting dishes, vacuuming. She tied the handle on a garbage bag, slipped into her flip-flops, and peered out the peephole in her door. Mr. DeVoss bungled his keys, dropped them, and grumbled to himself. The last thing she wanted this morning was a long, slow conversation with Mr. DeVoss. His door creaked open and thumped as he pulled it closed.

She opened her door, ready to sprint down to the back door, but Mr. DeVoss emerged carrying a box. She knocked into him, and his box clattered. "Oh my gosh."

She reached out as he fumbled with the box, losing his balance. The box clanked as the contents shifted. "Mother's china. Save it." He dropped to his knees.

"Mr. DeVoss, oh, no." Sif caught the box and hugged it to her chest as she reached for Mr. DeVoss, but he had already fallen on her garbage bag that burst with a whoosh of foul air.

He gave her a dazed look. "I'm—"

"I'm so sorry."

"Oh my. You saved the china." He reached out with his hand, and she pulled him to his feet.

"This was my fault."

"No, my dear. It's my fault. I need to slow down. I'm not as young as I once was." He took his hat off and rubbed his shiny pate.

Sif held the box. "But are you okay?"

He glanced at her with blank eyes, then nodded. "I need a moment to collect myself."

A whiff from the broken garbage bag hit her nostrils. "Oh. Pee-yew." She set the box down and retied the bag. "Mr. DeVoss. I'm so sorry. I was headed to the garbage bin and didn't even see you."

She waited for him to move, not sure what to do for him. "Why are you carrying a box of your mother's china?"

"What? Oh, I'm taking it to my sister. She's hosting the whole family and needs it to finish her table setting. When I host, she brings enough for me to—

"But you don't want to hear about my boring life. You must be busy grading papers and planning your classes."

She laughed. "Yes. The end-of-quarter stack is tall and waiting for me. Let's get you off the floor." She took his elbow, and helped him to his feet. He was light. "Why don't I carry the china, and you can carry my garbage bag. You were headed to your car, right?"

"What? Oh, yes, I am." He grunted, and she heaved until he was on his feet.

"Nothing broken or fractured?" she asked.

"What? Oh, no. I'm fine." To prove it, he touched his toes as he grabbed her garbage bag and grinned at her.

She nodded and lifted the box of China. They walked to the elevator. Mr. DeVoss never used the stairs. The elevator doors opened, and he motioned for her to enter. He didn't seem to limp or favor one leg over the other. They rode down in silence. Was he embarrassed? She was. The door opened, and she carried the china to his 1958 Volvo sedan. It was a classic, like him. She grinned.

"Here, let me help you with that." Roger materialized at her side, and she jumped. Where had he come from?

"Whoa. I'm not going to bite you." The look he gave her stopped her, and she chuckled.

"Of course not."

"Don't mind her," Mr. DeVoss said. "She probably doesn't want to run into anyone else today." He chuckled.

"Did you fall?" Roger frowned at Mr. DeVoss, then turned to Sif and arched an eyebrow.

Now she'd hear about it. All the things she should have done but didn't. Mr. DeVoss dropped the garbage bag and leaned on his car. She gasped but clutched the box of china. Roger reached for the elderly gentleman's elbow.

He ran a hand down Mr. DeVoss's arms and legs. "Are you dizzy?"

"What? No. I'm fine. Quit fussing." Mr. DeVoss tried to pull away, but Roger held his elbow.

Why hadn't she checked for bruises or sprains? As though she'd know what to do if she found something wrong.

"Good thing you're here, Doctor." She gave him a sheepish grin, but he didn't even glance at her. Was this what Nurse Gillian put up with? He was in another world, so focused on Mr. DeVoss she was invisible to him.

Roger took Mr. DeVoss's chin in his hand and gazed into his eyes. "Look left, right, now up and down. Are you feeling nauseous?"

"What? No. Not anymore." Mr. DeVoss brushed lint from his jacket lapel.

Roger released Mr. DeVoss's elbow, frowning at him. Sif shifted from foot to foot, unsure what to do.

"No pain is good. Any more dizziness?"

"Nope." Mr. DeVoss took Roger's hand and shook it. "Thanks, Doc, but I really must be on my way. My sister is expecting me with these dishes."

"Okay. You seem fine but call me if you develop any pain later."

Mr. DeVoss laughed. "Oh, please, I have eighty-one years of wear and tear and arthritis in every joint. There's always pain. I'm fine."

The older gentleman brushed his coat sleeves and adjusted his lapels, unlocked his car, and Sif put the box on the back seat. "It was nice running into you, Sif." He chuckled and waved as he started his car and backed out of his spot.

"He seems so frail." When had that happened? Sif kept him in sight as he drove out of the parking lot. She'd always avoided him because once he started talking, he didn't stop, but why couldn't she listen for ten minutes? "I should have…"

"Should have what? Given him an exam? Do you know how?" Roger grinned at her. "You did fine. He left with most of his dignity intact, so you did him a favor."

He stood with his hands on his hips, and she wanted to roll into a ball.

She ran her hand over her ponytail. "Should he be driving?" She picked up the garbage bag.

"That's not our call, thankfully. He has a sister, right? Any other family?"

"A brother, a couple of nephews and nieces and their kids. No wife, no kids of his own. Poor Mr. DeVoss. The only visitor I've ever seen is his sister." She stood with Roger, staring at the pier and the fishermen coming and going. Mr. DeVoss lived alone, just like she did. His life might be a foreshadowing of hers in fifty years if she wasn't careful. She glanced at Roger. He rocked on his heels, his hands in his pockets. Would he jingle his keys?

"Too bad. Must be lonely." He jingled his keys.

She grinned, then sighed. "Lonely. What a dreadful word."

Was Nurse Gillian waiting for Roger? Why didn't she just ask him if he was dating her too? She kicked a rock across the parking lot.

"Well, I have a stack of papers with my name on them, so I better run." She swung the garbage bag into the bin on her way inside.

Really? A stack of papers? Lame. Maybe she should go for a run instead. Was he watching her? She glanced over her shoulder, startled that he was. Was he checking out her butt?

She slumped against the doorframe inside the stairwell. Boris. He still undermined everything she did, but why did she let it happen? Sometimes there was no answer for "why." She wiped her nose on her sleeve. Roger's dark eyes were so—

She shuddered and jogged up the steps. The run could wait. She had to finish grading those papers today.

Lonely.

Her chest ached with loneliness, and she placed a hand over her heart. Would she grow old alone, like Mr. DeVoss? Maybe he'd been jilted, too?

Chapter 15

Boris?

Sif turned the knob on her front door. She only had five more papers, and today she would finish them, but all she wanted was to get out of these tight heels and into her running clothes. She put her key in the lock, but the door opened. Had she forgotten to lock again? She needed to pay attention.

She stepped inside and stumbled over a pair of shoes. Loafers? She gasped and crouched against the wall. Who was in the condo? Her heart lurched and her skin crawled.

"Who's there?" She reached into her purse for her phone.

"Hey, babe."

Sif dropped her phone, and it clattered on the floor. She clasped a hand to her chest.

Boris ambled barefoot down the hallway with Mr. Martini in his arms.

"Boris?"

The cat purred loud enough for her to hear, and she blinked. "What are you doing here?"

"I'm back, baby." He stood in his stockinged feet and grinned at her.

"Back?" She shook her head. A wave of nausea hit her. How had she found him irresistible? She couldn't breathe.

"Surprised?" He grinned and reached for her with one arm, the other cradling Martini, the purring, little traitor.

She glared at him and slapped his hand away. "How did you get in here? Where's Shirley?"

He frowned, and Martini jumped from his arms. "I kept a key, remember?"

"No. I don't remember." She reached for her phone. "I'm calling Nanc."

"Shirley stayed in Barbados, the tramp." Boris kept talking as though he hadn't heard her, and Martini slinked into the bedroom. "Aren't you happy to see me?"

"No. I'm not. You have to—" Sif held up a hand, but she couldn't stop him. He scooped her into his arms and pulled her to him. She wriggled against his embrace.

"Stop it." She pushed against his chest, but he clamped her to him and tried to kiss her. Something in her snapped, and she stomped on his bare instep and clapped both hands over his ears.

"Ow." He released her, putting one hand to an ear, the other to his foot.

"Keep your hands off me." She rushed past him into the condo.

He rubbed his foot. "What the hell? Babe?"

"This is not going to happen." Her heart raced as she ran to the kitchen.

Who did he think he was, breaking into her condo? She should have known he'd kept a key. She scanned the countertop for something, anything that might act as a weapon.

Knife? No.

She grabbed a meat mallet from the utensil container by the stove. Perfect. She raised it over her head as she ran down the hall. "Get out, get out, get out."

She swung the mallet. He held up an arm blocking the blow, but it connected with a crack.

"Ow. That hurt." He stepped back, cradling his arm.

"Good." She swung again, but he dodged to the left, and she fell forward.

"This is my condo too, remember? I'm the one who qualified for the loan." He frowned at her, holding up his hands to protect his head.

"Nanc warned me to get a restraining order, but I didn't listen." Sif swung the mallet.

Boris crouched, taking a blow to the shoulder. "Sif, stop."

She couldn't stop. She didn't want to stop. Her blood sang in her veins as she lifted the mallet. "You." She took a step back and sighed. "You—left me at the altar, remember?" She cradled the mallet to her chest.

"Let's be reasonable." He held his hands out to fend her off.

"Reasonable?" She stomped her foot.

A knock at the door startled her. She lowered the mallet, but Boris opened the door before she could stop him. Roger stood with his mouth open, his head swiveled to Sif, to the mallet, to Boris's bare feet. He frowned at the scene, and her heart sank. Did he think Boris was moving back in?

"I heard a commotion. Are you all right?" Roger took a step, but Boris grabbed his hand and shook it, keeping him outside.

"Everything's great. I'm Boris, her—" He paused. "—boyfriend." Boris glanced over his shoulder at Sif with a grin. He kept a tight grip on Roger's hand.

"You are not my—" Sif raised the mallet again. "You are Shirley's leftovers. Now get out."

"Sif, can't we talk about this? I have too much money tied up in this condo. I need it now, since Shirley—"

Roger jerked his hand from Boris's. "You heard her. She wants you to leave." But Boris didn't move.

Sif took a step. "Roger, I didn't know—" If she could just get to Roger, everything would be okay. She dropped the mallet to her side and glared at Boris.

Boris stood between her and Roger. The walls pressed in on her, and she longed for fresh air and Roger's arms around her.

Damn Boris.

"You wouldn't have this condo if not for me. You're barely making the payments, remember?" He threw up his hands. "My credit is shot full of holes, and Shirley's gone. I need someplace to stay." He took a step toward Sif, his hand outstretched.

She shook her head. What did she ever see in this jerk anyway? She took in his gray socks that were once white, his wrinkled shirt, his five-o'clock shadow, his stinky shoes. She tapped the mallet in her hand.

"I'm sure we can settle this in court if that's what you want, but you are not moving in."

Roger pushed Boris, but Boris spread his feet and didn't budge. "Listen, Roger, get lost."

Roger punched Boris in the belly, and he doubled over. Sif gasped and took a step back. Roger pushed past him and took Sif's elbow and stood towering over her, his warmth giving her strength.

Boris coughed and doubled over, holding his

stomach. "I have nowhere to go. I wouldn't have come, but this is my last option."

"I doubt that." Sif waved the mallet at Boris. He was ruining everything, but was there anything between her and Roger to ruin? She gritted her teeth and glared at Boris.

"Okay, I'll listen to your sad story, but Roger stays." Sif stomped down the hall. "And I'm calling Nanc. She's got to hear this."

"Wait." Boris stopped in the middle of the hall. "Nanc doesn't need to be part of this, and neither does he. We can work something out between just us, right, Sif?"

Sif sighed. "There is nothing to work out and nothing you can say to talk your way back into my life."

He was desperate, but how could he expect this from her? She wasn't giving up the condo. Yes, it was expensive, but he couldn't contest their agreement, could he? She took Roger's hand and walked into the living room. The view of Puget Sound spread out before her, as storm clouds gathered over the peninsula.

Boris's suit coat was draped over a dining room chair. She threw it on the floor and dragged the chair into the living room for Roger. He sat, and she sank into an upholstered chair across the coffee table from Boris. It was a face-off, and Sif gripped the arms of the chair. Boris was a "finisher." He made multimillion-dollar deals all the time, the slimeball. She'd have to be careful what she said.

She shook the mallet at him, then dialed Nanc.

"You should get your locks changed." Roger glared at Boris.

* * *

Boris shuffled out the door, and it clicked shut behind him. Sif scowled at his muddy footprints smudging her entry. What a jerk.

"Well, at least he's gone." Sif sighed. "But he'll be back."

"If I weren't on call tonight, I wouldn't leave you alone."

She couldn't speak. She wanted to curl into a ball against Roger's side and sleep for hours. She glanced up at him, and he took her in his arms. She sighed and pressed against him.

Boris made her stomach sick, but so did Nurse Gillian. Why couldn't she just ask him about his feelings? Because she was a big chicken, that's why.

"Call me if anything happens. Okay?" He pulled away, his shirt wet from her tears.

"I will." Sif wiped her eyes as she opened the door and closed it behind him.

He seemed sincere, and his knight-in-shining-armor act was a turn-on, but she hadn't taken him for the swoop-in-and-rescue-the-damsel-in-distress sort of guy. She dialed Nanc and slumped in a chair, staring out the window. Puget Sound spread before her, the water choppy and gray.

"Sif," Nanc's voice crooned over the speaker and filled the condo.

Sif shivered. "Oh, Nanc. I can't afford another court case on my teacher's salary. I should have known that this perfect little condo couldn't last. I already have to teach four classes a quarter just to make the payments, and now Boris—"

"I know it's not what you wanted to hear, but

listen, I have an accountant friend who's a financial planner. We should be able to salvage some equity. The housing market has boomed over the past year, and you should be able to walk away with…"

"That's the point, though. I don't want to walk away. I love this old building, the wainscot, the Tiffany lights, Elgin, the *Quatre* Hens, and the view. I don't want to live anywhere else." Sif sniffled.

"Oh, Sif—"

Sif hadn't added Roger to her list of reasons to stay, but was he going to stay, or was he taking that job in Colorado?

She sighed. "Dad told me never to get sentimental over real estate, but he never got sentimental over anything. It's too late. I am sentimental. My soul lives in these old walls, and Roger…"

"Roger is a good man, right?"

"I guess, but he'll probably be leaving soon with Nurse Gillian." Why had she said that?

"What? But I thought—"

"You didn't see what I saw." Her guts were churning, and she couldn't focus. "You think because he stood with me against Boris, he cared about me?"

"He does care for you. Anyone with eyes can see how he looks at you. Who's this Nurse—"

"Nanc, focus on the condo." She slumped into the chair with a sigh. "I have to save my home right now."

"I know. I'm sorry, but there—"

"Tell me the truth. Can I afford this place? I should have known reality would catch up with me." Her throat tightened as she spoke, but she didn't want to cry. She'd never solve this problem with tears.

Nanc's silence could only mean one thing. She was

angry. Sif braced herself.

"Your reality was to get married and live happily ever after, and Boris tied the financial knot with you, then left—

"Say, I just thought of something."

"What?" She sat forward in her chair. If anyone could help her, Nanc could.

"I'll call you later."

"Wait." Sif held the phone out, but Nanc was gone. Nanc's ideas came quick and sudden, and then she was gone, leaving Sif to stare at her phone.

"Classic Nanc, right, Martini?" She pulled the cat into her lap and stroked his luxurious fur. "What would we do without her or this condo?"

Or Roger, but she couldn't say that out loud.

She closed her eyes. Roger had learned more about her in the last half hour, and most of it she'd never wanted to share with anyone, especially him. Her head ached, and her old wounds bruised her anew.

Damn Boris.

Her legs ached, probably from too much sitting. She stood, letting the cat jump to the floor. He meowed and rubbed against her leg.

"Sorry, kid, but it's time for a run. I'll just cry myself into a migraine, sitting around here."

She headed to the closet and pulled out running shoes and a fleece. It would take at least five miles to clear her head. She pulled on her leggings.

"Crap." She hadn't asked Boris for his key.

Chapter 16

Grading Papers

She sat at the dining room table and picked up a paper. She read the first line, but she couldn't focus. The words blurred. She read the first paragraph three times. Grading papers left her drained these days, but why? If she had known how exhausting teaching was, would she still have gotten her master's and walked, terrified, into that first classroom?

Yes. Of course, she would.

She squinted at the screen, but her phone vibrated. She glanced at it and groaned, dropping her head in her hands.

Boris.

Again.

A scream rose in her throat, but she swallowed it down. He did it on purpose, like one of Mom's sheep, leaning on the fence day after day until it finally broke. This was harassment. She forwarded all of Boris's texts to Nanc, who transcribed them as she prepared the restraining order. Nanc and Boris's lawyer did all the communicating, but Boris still poked her with these annoying texts.

She dialed Mom. *Pick up, please pick up.*

"Hello, baby."

"Mom, Boris showed up."

"What? When?"

"A couple of days ago."

"And you're just telling me this now?"

"You're busy, and—"

"Not that busy. What did he want?"

"The condo, Mom. He wants the condo. It was horrible, and Roger showed up—" Sif glanced out at the Sound.

"Boris and Roger? In your condo? That must have been fun. Why is that deranged idiot back?"

"Shirley dumped him, and he needs someplace to stay because apparently his credit is trashed, so he can't even rent an apartment. I might lose the condo, Mom."

"Oh, Sif. Did you call Nanc?"

"Yes. She's a lifesaver. She's working on an idea. I don't know all the details yet, but…"

"Nanc is one of the smartest young women I know, after you, of course. She'll get you the justice you deserve."

Sif ran her fingers through her hair. "Thanks, Mom, but I don't feel very smart right now."

"Well, you are smart, and I won't hear a word otherwise. I'm so sorry about Boris. What a nightmare."

"Thanks. I needed to hear you say that." She sighed and rested her head in her hand, her elbow braced on the table. "Say, any decision on Christmas?"

"Didn't I tell you? Betty Boop delivered her lamb early. They are both confined in the barn, under constant observation. You know, small meals every couple of hours. It's so tiny it can hardly stand without falling down, so fingers crossed."

"Poor Betty Boop's lamb. I'm sorry. I know how much you care about every animal on your farm." She sighed. "Text me a progress report."

"Will do, honey. Good luck with Boris, and I'll keep you posted on Christmas. Just tell Ellen yes, and we'll think positive."

"Thanks, Mom. Love you." Sif rubbed her tired eyes.

Mom was too distracted to fully commit, Sif could relate to being distracted, but what about family? Sif needed her too. She wasn't going to get her, though. Thank heavens for Nanc. She'd accepted without a pause.

She glanced at the last four papers on the table. They were going to have to wait. She couldn't read another paragraph, let alone a ten-pager. Why did the end of the quarter always leave her flattened?

She pinched the bridge of her nose, but the headache pinched back. Was Roger packing for Colorado, or did he even unpack? She pushed Roger from her mind, jumped up, and marched to her closet. A quick run to clear her head, then she'd finish grading.

****

Sif pumped her arms to the rhythm of her breath, her brain fog lifting with each stride. Nothing like salty air to perk her up. She sprinted through the park, then walked the last half mile home. Fluffy clouds floated overhead, one shaped like Mickey Mouse, another a cat's head, another a VW bug. Or was it a turtle?

She passed two women and a Yorkie strolling down the middle of the trail. Tires crunched over the gravel, warning her someone was pulling into the parking lot. Roger stopped his red Camry and idled in the middle of the lot. She stopped. Why didn't he park? All she wanted was a shower and to get back to grading. Could she sneak by him?

He held his phone to his ear, nodding. Who was he talking to, Nurse Gillian? Colorado? Sweat trickled down her back, and a seagull squawked right above her.

This was ridiculous. Was she going to stand here and sweat? No. She needed a shower. If she detoured to the front door, he wouldn't even notice her.

"Sif, hey."

Or not. She spun around but did not smile. Roger's grin dissolved as he walked up to her. Would he tell her about his good news from Colorado? She put a hand to her heart. She had made the mistake of letting him in. He never intended to stay here. Why would he?

"Roger." She forced a smile to her lips, but a familiar pounding started in her temple.

"You're going to the Christmas dinner, right?" He shoved his hands in his pockets.

Was he asking her to be his date? She cleared her throat so she could speak. "I am."

"Good." He blocked her escape to the condo.

Sif clenched her fists. Was that all he had to say? This was anything but good. Why didn't he just spit it out? He was leaving, and why did Sif still care? She had no hold on Roger. He'd kissed Nurse Gillian, hadn't he?

"I have to get back to work. Bye." She squeezed around him and with a small wave darted inside.

She unlocked her condo door and slumped in a heap in the entry. Sniffling, she brushed at her eyes wet with tears. Mr. Martini rubbed against her knee, and she pulled him into her arms and buried her face in his silky fur. "Oh, Martini. Did I let my guard down again? You're supposed to stop me from doing that, remember?"

****

Sif typed in her final comments at the end of the last research paper and entered the grade in her gradebook. She let the lightness of completing the biggest read of the quarter pull her out of the chair. She did this every quarter, but the exhilaration of finishing always left her giddy. She stood and stretched. Mr. Martini rubbed against her leg, and she reached for him, his purring chest vibrating against hers.

"I've been neglecting you, haven't I, Martini? Well, I'm done with all this grading nonsense, right?" Martini purred and kneaded the leg of her fuzzy pink pajamas.

Her doorbell rang. She set Martini on the floor and peered through the peephole. Mabel stood in the hall. She pulled the door open.

"It's only been a week. Should you be climbing stairs?" Sif frowned at Mabel, taking her elbow.

"I took the elevator, and don't take my arm. I'm not an invalid, yet." Mabel pulled away from Sif. "We need to have words." She marched into Sif's condo.

"Come in. I'll make tea." Sif followed her as she ambled to the comfy chair by the window. Sif's laptop sat open on the table, her college homepage open.

"That looks familiar."

Sif grinned. "I just finished grading the final paper. It's all over except for the class reflections."

Mabel had retired from teaching twenty years ago, but she could recall details that baffled Sif. Sif didn't have to explain anything to Mabel. She had experienced the satisfaction of getting all the grading done.

"Any good paper topics this quarter?" Mabel let

Martini jump into her lap, and his purrs shook his body. Sif put the water on for tea.

"I got an interesting analysis of one of August Wilson's plays and then a very informative explication on solar energy."

She let the water splash into the kettle. This life wasn't so bad. She'd be fine without Roger, right? She had Mabel, her work, Martini, and this condo, for the moment, at least.

Sif sank into the chair opposite Mabel and tucked her legs under her. "I had one on Cleopatra. Did you know she wasn't even Egyptian, and she married her own brother?"

Mabel laughed. "As a matter of fact, I did. You learn as much as your students, don't you? I miss that."

"Hopefully they learn a thing or two from me too, but I always enjoy their topics."

"So." Mabel examined her fingernails. "How's Roger?"

"Roger?" She sank farther in the chair and frowned. Mabel too? She'd just finished grading papers. Mabel wouldn't ask unless something was up. She gripped the arms of her chair.

"Don't give me that wounded bird look, Sif. We've all seen the two of you together. He cares about you, and you care about him, and with Boris harassing you, wouldn't it be good to have—"

Sif held up her hand and shook her head. "I don't need a man to save me, Mabel. I can deal with Boris, and let Roger worry about his new job in Colorado."

It was Mabel's turn to grip the arms of her chair. "Colorado? He's leaving?"

"To take his dream job. He can carpool with that

traveling nurse, Gillia—"

"Nurse Gillian? You do have some strange ideas, but you're wrong this time." Mabel pushed herself to a stand. "She throws herself at him, yes, but she throws herself at every eligible doctor at the hospital and some of the nurses."

She did? This was news. What else did Mabel know about Nurse Gillian?

The tea kettle whistled, and Sif stood. Saved by the bell. "Have you heard from Elgin?"

"Don't you change the topic, missy." Mabel glared at Sif. "That little skank Gillian is about as interesting to Doctor Roger Dodger as yesterday's med charts."

Sif put a hand over her mouth. Mabel was too furious to put up with her laughter, but she was so cute when she got mad. Besides, Roger would probably be fascinated by yesterday's med charts, knowing him.

She poured water over the tea bags in her Rose Chintz teapot. "Skank? Do tell and don't hold back. You must have all the dirt."

"I know that she's young and doesn't want to settle down because she loves to travel. Her time here is almost up, and she just wants to have a good time while she's here. Roger is too smart to let her turn his head." Mabel crossed her arms. "If you can't see that, you're blind."

Sif laughed. "All I know is Roger and I had some nice moments." She paused.

Some very nice moments, but that's all they were. But he was leaving. She brushed tea leaves from her fingers. "Right now, I have to figure out how I'm going to afford this condo so I can stay with my friends." She smiled at Mabel but took a step back. Mabel shook her finger at her.

"You're making the biggest mistake of your life."

Sif sighed and opened her mouth, but Mabel cut her off.

"Roger fell for you the moment he met you, and you fell for him. We all saw it happen, and we were so happy for you. You pushed all your feelings down after Boris, and when Roger got here you blossomed, but now Boris is back—"

Mabel put a hand to her throat.

"Are you ok—"

"I'm fine." Mabel glared at her. "Don't blow this, Sif. Roger's a keeper."

"A keeper? What are you talking about?" Sif stood with her hands on her hips. Mabel sounded like Dad. He'd said that marrying Boris would be a disaster. Why hadn't she listened to him? And what would he think of Roger?

"Roger will not leave you at the altar."

Sif crossed her arms. "We're not getting married." She glared at Mabel, who stood with her arms crossed, glaring back.

Stalemate. Sif would not be duped by yet another man. "I have to check my final grades and post them, Mabel, so if you'll excuse me."

"Forget about tea, but don't forget what I said, got it?" Mabel huffed and stomped to the door.

Chapter 17

Sif Gets Tough

Sif tied her running shoes, and Martini meowed by the door.

"Yes, I'm going out, and no, you can't come. Back, back, back, back, you little escape artist."

She patted his head, then squeezed out the door. He thought he was a dog, but if he got out—

She shuddered. If he got out, she'd never find him. She couldn't let that happen. She speed-walked along the porch and jogged down the stairs to the back door. She'd call that her warm-up and hit the park running.

She burst through the door, and a glint of red shone in the parking lot. Her heart lurched. Roger. What was he doing home already?

He did live here, so there was that, and he waved, so she'd been seen. She stood with her arms hanging by her sides. He smiled as he pulled into Elgin's spot and jumped from his car. Should she ask him how Nurse Gillian was? No. It was none of her business. She clenched her fists.

"Hey, want a running partner? If you give me five minutes, I could be ready."

Was he clueless, or was she? She'd seen him kissing Nurse Gillian. Mabel had called her a skank, though. But he was taking the Colorado job, the jerk. She shook her head and pulled her phone out to check the time.

"Sorry, but I can't wait. I'm swamped with grading." She'd turned in her grades yesterday, yet the lie rolled out of her mouth so easily. Did her face give her away?

"Oh. Okay." He jangled his keys in his pocket, his bottom lip pouting.

Hmm. Pouty lip was sexy, but still. She scanned the parking lot for something to throw at him, but all she had were her house keys, and he'd probably take that as an invitation.

She clenched her teeth and jogged across the street, picking up her pace as she hit the running path. Maybe she should have thrown her keys.

No. Be strong, Sif. Be strong.

****

Birds twittered in the branches as Sif walked out of the park. She waited for a car before crossing the street, wiping sweat from her brow. A good run always made her problems disappear. She unlocked the front door and climbed the stairs, but Roger's voice stopped her.

She peered over the railing. He stood in the porch in front of Elgin's condo dressed in jogging pants, his hoodie zipped to his chin. He gazed at the road with a vacant stare as he held his phone to his ear.

"Yes. I am still interested. I've always wanted to be part of the work you do. Yes, I did complete my internship at the U of C Hospital, so I know it well. Mm-hmm. Mm-hmm. Okay. I'll call next week with my decision. Thank you."

Sif gasped and backed from the railing to the wall. So, it was true. He was going for the Colorado job. This was no surprise, so why did a pain shoot through her chest? She blinked back tears and put a hand to her face. That's what the kiss was about. Nurse Gillian was going with him.

She peered over the railing, but he'd left for his run. Her breath caught in her throat. He was really leaving, just like Boris. No. Not like Boris. Roger was never staying.

She wiped her eyes on her sleeve. "Stop crying. You're tough, right? Besides, the last thing you need is a relationship right now." She ran up the stairs and flew into her apartment before her sobs could escape.

The last thing she needed were the *Quatre* Hens checking on her.

A knock on the door startled her. How long had she been sitting here? She wiped her eyes and opened the door.

"Did I hear weeping?" Mr. DeVoss shuffled his feet and wrung his hands, his discomfort painful. "Are you all right?"

Of course he'd heard weeping. Who was she kidding? She forced a smile.

"Oh, it must have been my TV. I'm watching the Hallmark Channel."

He cocked his eyebrow. Her TV wasn't even on, and he frowned. She wiped her eyes, cursing Colorado and Nurse Gillian. They were taking Roger.

"Of course, my dear. I blame my old ears." He gave a small bow and shuffled to his door. "Have a good evening."

She couldn't imagine the Cliff Edge Condos without Roger, but she was going to have to. Heat rose to her neck and into her cheeks.

Damn Colorado. She shut her door and leaned

against it with a sigh. She had to pull herself together. No one else was going to catch her crying.

****

Sif checked her weather app. Sunset was at 4:19 p.m. today. How depressing. She sat at the dining room table. Dinner alone, again. One of her students' research papers said that eating alone was linked to depression, so she was screwed. She ate alone most nights.

She unlocked the door and wandered onto the porch. Voices echoed through the air, but the rolled *r*'s were Trudy's. The *Quatre* Hens had cornered someone. A man's voice mumbled something. Roger? She peeked over the porch banister.

He stood, hands in the air to fend off the Hens as they stood before him. He had his back against the door to Elgin's condo, and Linda was jabbing her finger at his chest.

"You need to tell her the truth about Nurse Gillian," Linda said.

So, he was dating Nurse Gillian? Sif clamped a hand over her mouth. She never should have said yes to that first date. Would she ever be able to date again?

Damn Boris.

"If you don't, we will." Mabel shook a fist at him.

"You can't leave without talking to her," Ellen said.

"Doctor Roger Dodger, don't hurt our Sif." Trudy's voice shook.

Too late for that. Why hadn't Mabel stopped them? Sif sighed. They didn't have to protect her. Done was done.

The quarter was over, and she wanted to celebrate

with a single-serving gluten-free veggie pizza she didn't have to share. And no more tears. She eased the front door closed and leaned on it.

What truth could they possibly want him to tell her, though? That he loved Nurse Gillian. Sif didn't need to hear that. Fresh tears rolled down her cheeks, but she didn't have the energy to wipe them away.

****

The waves were tossing a small cruiser as it bobbed toward the marina. The lights on the pier glistened off the rough water, illuminating the boat. Who would venture out in this storm? Rain trickled down the window as she nibbled toast and sipped her hot cocoa. She held her warm mug to her lips, inhaled the mellow aroma of chocolate.

Her phone rang. "Nanc. Of course, I'm home. Where are you?" She hit speaker and, taking a sip of cocoa, sank back in the chair.

Nanc's voice filled her living room with cheer. "I'm Christmas shopping. We only have four days, in case you've forgotten. Have you bought my present yet?" Nanc's chuckle tinkled through the room. "Don't tell me you baked my gift again."

Sif grinned despite her dark mood. "Okay. I don't want to spoil the surprise." Nanc was good at drawing her out and back into life. "Are you buying something nice to wear to the feast? The *Quatre* Hens are expecting you in all your Christmas glory."

Sif kept the boat in sight until it rounded the jetty and motored into the marina and calm water. She sheltered in Nanc's optimism from the Boris-storm he was brewing over this condo. She couldn't lose the condo, not now that she'd found herself, her strength.

115

Losing Roger was a blow. He'd seemed perfect, but Nurse Gillian had opened her eyes.

"What did you get Roger?" Nanc huffed and puffed as she spoke.

"Are you in Seattle? Sounds like you're climbing a hill."

"I'm headed home, and don't avoid my question."

"Why would I get Roger something? We aren't even dating."

"Of course you are. Everyone knows that except for you, apparently. I haven't seen you this excited over a guy, well, since—"

Sif jumped out of the chair. "Nanc, Roger is taking the job in Colorado, and Nurse Gillian is going with him. I overheard everything." Tears streamed down her face.

"No. You're wro—"

"Any news on the condo?" Sif blinked. She was not going to cry.

"Not definitive news, but we both know Boris doesn't have a case. I heard he went back to Shirley and was trying to schmooze her to let him move in." Nanc chuckled. "But she brought some scuba instructor back with her."

Sif grinned. "Figures. Not very bright, is he? Listen, I gotta go."

"Okay, but call me later?"

"Sure." Sif ended the call. She'd gotten Nanc off the Roger rant this time, but she'd bring him up again.

Boris. What an idiot, but she didn't care about him anymore. She could thank Roger for that.

Roger.

She sighed and gazed out the window. Darkness

had settled over Puget Sound, accentuating the lights of a steamship loaded with cargo.

Chapter 18

Christmas Wish Knotts

Snow was in the forecast, and Sif grinned as she opened her storage unit door.

"Cross-country skiing, here we come." She pulled her skis out along with her poles.

Her dad always said, "Only one reason to go skiing." And she'd always finish, "Because it's snowing."

Boris skied like a pro. She shook her head. *Don't go there.* She needed this solo test, and she needed the cardio. The fresh mountain air would energize her and pull her out of this funk.

She grabbed her ski boots and put the skis and poles over her shoulder. She backed out of her storage unit as Roger locked the door of Elgin's condo.

"Damn." She bit her bottom lip. He had impeccable timing, but he was in running shoes. Maybe he'd jet to the park without noticing her.

He turned and stopped, a smile spreading over his face. He had no shame, that man, but still her heart raced.

"You ski? How did I not know that? Look at those shiny, red beauties." He ran his hand down the length of her skis. "We should plan a trip up sometime." He reached out to take the skis from her.

Fine. She'd let him navigate the corners with her

long skis if he wanted to. "I'm sure you are way too busy to go skiing with me." She stared at her boots.

He grinned. "I'll make time."

His windblown hair draped across his forehead, and the twinkle in his eye made her blush.

"My grandma taught me to ski when I was six. We skied together until two years ago." Why did she bring up Grandma? Was she a glutton for doom and gloom?

"She must have been some grandma." He chuckled.

He'd used past tense, and she nodded. At least she didn't have to explain her death. She'd passed just before the wedding debacle. Sif glanced at him from downcast eyes.

"She was amazing. A great athlete and my biggest supporter. I miss her."

"Is that why you get along with the *Quatre* Hens so well?" He put her skis on her ski rack.

She frowned. Was it? She tightened the straps in the ski rack. "Maybe. I try to see people, not their age, and the Quatre Hens welcomed me at a time when I really needed friends. My grandma would have chased Boris down and kicked his butt." She chuckled.

"Wow. Go Grandma." He smiled. "Where are you headed?"

"To a forest service road up 410. It's quiet and beautiful."

He shook his head. "You know, you shouldn't go into the backcountry alone. Next time, I'm going with you. Do you have your avalanche beacon?"

"Geez. Yes, Dad." She frowned as she threw her boots in the back and closed the door. Did he just invite himself to go skiing? "Well, I guess I'll see you at the

Christmas dinner tomorrow."

"Yep." She shut her door and started her car, backing out before she buckled in, and he could give any more advice.

She turned on the radio, and the quick melody of "The Twelve Days of Christmas" filled the car.

"This is what I need, a little Christmas music and some fun in the snow." She adjusted her rearview mirror and caught Roger's reflection.

What was with the long face? She let the music lift her spirits. No oncoming cars, so hhe pulled onto the road. *Don't glance back, Sif.* She glanced in the mirror one last time, and her heart fluttered. He was still watching.

****

The doorbell rang. Sif sighed and grabbed her crutches. One fall, and she was out for the season. At least she'd slipped after her trek and near her car, but why hadn't she taken her skis off before she got to the car?

Done is done. She couldn't undo the fall or the fractured ankle. With a grunt, she rose and maneuvered down the hall. She opened her front door, leaning on the crutches.

Mom hugged her, the scent of wood fires and fresh straw rising from her coat. "Honey, I'm so sorry." Mom kissed her cheek. "It's like this every time. You're healthy all quarter then have a catastrophe during your vacation."

Sif shrugged.

"Mm. Something smells good."

Sif hobbled back down the hallway. "Bean casserole for the feast. It has fifteen more minutes." She sighed. Was it the fractured ankle that got Mom's attention? At least she was here.

"It's like the universe knows I'm on break and can take a little adventure. Remember the year I got jury duty at Christmas?"

"I do." Mom nodded. "Supreme court in downtown Seattle."

"There was no getting out of that one, but it turned out to be fascinating—" She plopped in a chair by the window.

"Attempted murder, right? You get called for jury duty more than anyone I know, but you do your civic duty." Mom beamed at her, and a warm glow filled Sif. Mom leaned down and kissed her forehead. "My daughter, making the world a better place."

"I don't know about that."

"Wow! Look at this place. Have you painted since I was here last?" Mom ran her hand over the fireplace mantel and stopped in front of the picture window. "Ahh. This view and all the built-ins. They don't build places like this anymore." Mom ran her fingers over the book spines in the built-in bookshelves. A fire glowed in the gas fireplace.

"It's been a while since you were here, but the view hasn't changed, has it?" Sif rubbed her sore ankle. What a pain. It kept her captive in this condo with too much time to think. She couldn't wallow, though, not today.

She stared at Mom's profile. When had the gray hair started taking over? Handel's *Messiah* played in the background.

Mom plopped in a chair. "No wonder you have to teach extra classes." Mom grinned at her. "It's worth it, though. Just think. Boris is gone."

"Really, Mom? Way to ruin my Christmas buzz."

"I heard Shirley dumped him in Tahiti."

"It was Barbados, and he's back. I told you he showed up here at the condo, right?" Sif rested her head against the back of the chair and grinned.

"That's right. How could I forget?" Mom sat forward in the chair.

"You're always so busy with your sheep." She pouted. "*I* need you, Mom. And to top it off, I was still grading final papers." She was whining, but she didn't care. Mom brought it up.

"I'm so sorry, honey. I've been AWOL, what with Betty Boop and all the milking. We delivered our first order of skyr to the co-op last week, though." She ran her fingers through her hair. She glanced at Sif, her brown eyes warm and soft, and Sif held the gaze like a warm mug of chocolate after a long day in the snow.

"I'm here now." Mom tilted her head. "Tell me everything."

"There's not much to tell, really." The drain of fighting legal battles with Boris, mixed with the pain of her ankle, wore her out. "Where do I begin?"

"At the beginning, of course."

She sighed. "I opened the front door, and his loafers were in the middle of my entry. He tried to kiss me, Mom." She shuddered. "Next thing you know, I grabbed a mallet and was screaming 'get out.' That's what brought Roger to my door."

"Perfect timing. I need to meet this Roger guy."

"He'll be at the dinner, but don't get too excited. He's leaving for a job in Colorado after Christmas."

"Oh, no. I thought something was brewing between

you two?"

"I did, too, but it never came to a boil." Who was she kidding? She'd been boiling since she met him in the parking lot. Why did she have such bad luck with guys?

She cleared her throat. "You know, when Boris first left, I wished for him to dump Shirley, but I never dreamed she'd dump him, or that he'd show up at my door.

He's not getting the condo, though, not after the wedding debacle." Sif bit her lip. Handel's "Hallelujah Chorus" rose to a crescendo, filling the condo with its urgency. Sif snorted at the irony. It could be the soundtrack for her entire year.

"I know you never wanted revenge, but this is karma on a grand scale, or would you rather call it poetic justice?" Mom grinned and sank onto the matching chair.

Mom made no secret of not liking Boris. Not to his face, but she'd warned Sif before the wedding. Why hadn't she listened?

She stared at the lights on the far shore. Even with gray hair, Mom seemed younger than her age, with her athletic build and strong will.

Sif laid her head back in the chair. These were the moments she relished with her mom, her quiet, calm presence where she said just the right things. It's what made her a good shepherd for her flock.

Sif rubbed her eyes. They stung, but she hadn't cried over Boris for days, and she didn't even want to begin crying over Roger. Well, she'd cry a little, but it hardly mattered now. He was history, or soon would be, but that wrench in her belly. Was it over him leaving?

She reached her arms over her head in a long stretch. She better change the subject, or she would cry. "So, Johnson Homestead delivered its first order of skyr?"

Her mom glowed. "I like the sound of that. Johnson Homestead." She beamed. "We delivered right on schedule, and like I said, Betty Boop's delivery was rough, but we got through it, and the new sign was installed at the road the day before we delivered, so it's official."

"Congratulation, Mom, you'll need that sign because no one can see your farm through all those trees."

"The trees stay." Mom shook a finger at her.

"I agree." She raised her hands in submission and chuckled.

"By the way, how's your cankle?"

"My what?"

"You know. When your ankle swells and blends with your calf? *Calf* plus *ankle* equals *cankle*." Mom loved urban slang, but this one was a bit much, even for her.

"Good one." Sif adjusted in the chair to ease a jolt of pain, but she couldn't let on, or Mom would put her to bed, and she'd miss the feast. "My 'cankle' is fine."

Mom reached into her bag and, with a flourish, presented Sif with a gift box wrapped in Santa paper with a red bow. "A measure of our success, I brought you some fresh skyr."

"Does everything have to have a Norse twist?"

"It's our heritage, so yes." She grinned.

Sif hugged the present to her chest. "It's heavy. I'm honored. It will be like eating pure gold, with all the time you've put into this." She'd eaten Grandma's skyr as a child, but did she like it? She gave her mom a smile. "It probably needs to go in the fridge, right?"

"It does." Mom took the gift and headed to the kitchen. "Dinner is at six, right? We should probably head out soon. With your cankle, we'll have to allow for extra time, and your elevator is the slowest one I've ever ridden."

"It has character, besides the fact that it's almost a hundred years old." Sif rose from the chair with a grunt and hobbled a couple steps, pain shooting up to her hip. Mom grabbed her elbow, and Sif grunted as she adjusted the crutches under her arm. "You're right. It might take fifteen minutes to get to the club room." She sighed and wiped her brow, then grinned. "I guess we'd better go. We don't want to be late. Mabel gets cranky if people are tardy."

"It's the teacher in her." Mom put her arm around Sif. "So, tell me how you fractured your ankle, again."

"I fell on an icy spot. My ski went one way and my foot another. It felt like a tear."

"Oh, honey."

"I was alone, so I had to ski out, which took forever."

"Alone? I thought you knew better than that." Her mom frowned. "What if you'd broken a bone?"

"I didn't break anything." She frowned. Did she have to ratchet up the mom dial right now? "You'll laugh at this. It was on the tiniest hill ever. Figures, right? I wasn't paying attention, and my ankle took the brunt of the fall."

"Are you sure nothing's broken?"

"The doctor took X-rays. It's a sprain, but the drive to urgent care was not pleasant even so." She rested her ortho-boot on the floor, leaning on her crutches. A timer went off. "Great. That's my bean casserole."

"I'll wrap it in a couple towels." Mom took the casserole out of the oven and placed it in a basket with towels for insulation. "Mm. I just love the smells of a Christmas feast. And what might these be?" She lifted a cookie tin and shook it.

"I call them Christmas Wish Knotts. They're the Shakespeare Knotts, remember? Nanc changed the name to Good Luck Knotts after the wedding deb—"

"Of course, I remember the Shakespeare Knotts, but no need to mention that day." She sniffed the tin. "Did you do something different? I smell orange."

"Try one."

Mom popped the lid. She lifted a cookie and bit into it. She closed her eyes. "Mm. Oh baby, the orange zest is sublime."

"I thought the orange would give it a festive flair."

"It does." Her mom brushed her hands on her jeans and handed Sif the tin. "So, will this Roger guy be there? Linda and Trudy—"

"Whatever they said doesn't matter. Roger will be there, but he's coming with someone else, and he's leaving for Colorado after the New Year."

"I'm sorry—" Mom lifted the basket with both hands and held it away from her.

"Me too, but oh well." Sif gripped the tin and hobbled to the door. Was she headed into a Christmas minefield of emotions? Most likely.

****

Mom held the door, and Sif hobbled into the club room. A warm hand took her elbow. Startled, she pulled away with a wobble and glanced up.

Roger. She should have known. He knew how much pain her ankle gave her, but did he know he was making it worse? Nurse Gillian's laughter rang through the room like broken crystal.

Sif ground her teeth. She could do this. Smile her best Christmas smile and pretend nothing was wrong. Sif bit her bottom lip. Roger should go hold Gillian's hand.

"Want me to look at that ankle later?"

Sif snorted. "You mean my cankle?"

"Your what, now?" Roger bent to put a hand on her ankle.

She pulled her leg back. "No. It's Christmas, and you're off duty, remember?"

Linda swept up to Sif and twirled in her Christmas square dance skirt. Sif grinned. Linda held out her hands, and Sif placed the cookie tin in them. Linda opened the lid.

"Oh, Sif. You've outdone yourself. They're beautiful, so colorful. Look, Roger. Christmas Wish Knotts, two for each of the twelve days of Christmas." She chuckled at her joke and twirled away with the cookies.

Trudy stood at the record player and placed the needle on a record. The scratches lent it charm as a French children's choir sang "Silent Night" in French.

Roger hadn't left Sif's side, and she glared at him. "My mom wants to meet you."

"She does?" Was that a gleam in his eye? Shouldn't he be worried?

"Hmph." She glanced at Mom, who smiled and nodded. No escape this time.

"Well, I want to meet her too." He grinned and

jiggled his keys.

Why were his teeth so white? And that thick, dark hair and the way it hung over his forehead…

She adjusted her crutches. "Come on. Let's get this over with." Sif hobbled around chairs. Roger tried to help, but she was able to weave in and out of chairs and tables enough ahead of him to stay out of his reach.

She was breathless by the time she reached Mom, and she rested her foot on the floor.

"Mom, this is Roger." He made a low bow.

"Roger. Mabel was just telling me all about you." Mom grabbed his hand and shook hard. Roger's whole body jerked.

"Wow." Roger rubbed his shoulder and winked at Sif. "That's quite a handshake."

Mabel laughed and put a hand to her chest.

Roger frowned at her. "Do I need to escort you to a chair, madam?"

"Oh, Doctor Roger." Mabel swatted a hand at him. He had all the *Quatre* Hens wrapped around his little finger.

"Excuse me." Sif nodded, turned, and limped to Nanc standing by the window. The lights twinkled off the water in a festive glow. She wanted to complain about Roger.

Nanc pointed to the north. "Here comes the Christmas ship." The colorful ship was festive and cruising toward the marina. "What do you think they'll sing tonight? 'Jingle Bells'?"

"I'm hoping for 'O Holy Night,' my favorite." Sif put her arm around Nanc, and they leaned on one another.

"Roger turned down the job. Did you know?"

Sif jerked back. "He what? No. I heard him—"

She shook her head, speechless. Nanc's words had come to her so soft and quiet, but they hit her like a sledgehammer.

"Did he tell you that?" Sif stared at Nanc.

"Nope. Nurse Gillian did. She is leaving for her next gig in Boston, so her apartment is all packed up, no pots or pans to cook with. That's the only reason he invited her."

"But? I tho—"

"I know you did, and therein lies the problem." Nanc took her by the shoulders and gave her a shake. "You over analyze everything."

"I can't believe it." Sif clung to Nanc, or she'd have fallen.

"Sometimes you need to quit thinking and just open your eyes. He turned down the job so he could stay here with you." Nanc glared at her.

"What do I do?"

"You fix this, whatever this is, by talking to him. Now go get that man. Stat."

Sif brushed hair strands from her face. He wasn't leaving with Nurse Gillian? She had misread the hugs and the flirting. He was just helping her out, and Mabel had been right, but she didn't listen to her either.

She raised her unsteady hand to her lips and slumped against the wall. "What have I done?"

"I'm not sure, but there's still time to fix it." Nanc gave her a nudge.

The ships colorful lights blinked, filling the room with cheer, and someone's laughter jangled her nerves. Could she fix this? Was that why Roger was so oblivious? Because he was innocent?

Damn Boris. He'd broken her trust-o-meter.

She glanced at Nanc. "I've been so horrible to him…"

She craned her neck, searching the room. The promise of roast turkey filled the air, and her tummy rumbled. She rubbed her face with her hands. Roger wasn't Boris. She'd lost sight of the differences between them. "I don't see him."

"He's still talking to your mom." Nanc took Sif by the hand. "All he thinks about is you. The scolding he got from the *Quatre* Hens made him back off, and he wanted to give you time to get over Boris, then Boris showed up. It's been a crazy couple of weeks, you know?" Nanc shrugged and shook her head.

Sif shook her head. He wasn't leaving?

Nanc took her hands and held them tight. "He's a great guy, and if you don't get over there right now, I'm going to throw you over my shoulder and carry you." Nanc grabbed one of the crutches. "Or take these so you can't go anywhere while I bring him to you."

"No. I'll go." Sif wobbled. She closed her eyes and reached for Nanc. A strong hand gripped her arm, and she opened her eyes. Roger stood next to her, gazing down at her. Speak of the devil.

She clung to him. Was she gasping? Her body shook from the pounding of her heart. This was her chance. She inhaled and gave him a shaky smile. He took her hand and cradled her elbow. So far, so good. He stroked her arm, and tingles warmed her skin.

Trudy knocked on the table. "Shh, everyone, it's time for the tree-lighting."

She smiled up at Roger. She could tell him after. The room dimmed, and lights on the distant shore twinkled off the water and reflected on the ceiling. The scratch of the needle hitting the vinyl on Trudy's phonograph was the only sound. The notes of "Stille Nacht" filled the room. Roger pulled her into the curve at his side, and his warmth and the melody melted any apprehension she'd had.

Trudy counted. "*Un, deux, trois.*" She flipped a switch, and the tree lights sprang into brilliant and sparkling colors. Everyone clapped, and Elgin cried, "Bravo, ladies!"

Roger put his lips to her ear and whispered, "We need to talk."

"Oh." Sif put a hand to her mouth. He'd taken the words right out of her mouth. Was he going to tell her he was staying? Goose bumps ran up her arms and across her shoulders.

He grinned at her. Whatever it was that he wanted to say, it could wait. The magic of the colorful tree, the music, the feast laid on the buffet, the tantalizing aroma of roast turkey—all brought tears to her eyes.

Roger held her tighter, and she let herself mold against his chest. Across the room, she spied Nanc air-clapping, and Sif grinned back. Mom did a thumbs-up, and Mabel folded her hands in front of her and smiled. Was everyone in on her private moment? Did Roger see all this? She glanced up at him, his dark eyes bottomless.

"Everyone." Mabel tapped her wineglass with her spoon. "Trudy and I would like to make a toast."

Roger released her. "I like your mom." His warm breath caressed her cheek. "She has an impressive handshake."

"Yeah, she's a farm girl, for sure." She nodded.

Trudy glared at them and held a finger to her lips.

Roger nudged her. "Did we just get in trouble?"

Sif chuckled. She glanced around the table. So much happiness surrounded her. Mom's sheep were producing skyr. The *Quatre* Hens had Mabel back. Elgin was retiring his cane. Nanc had saved her condo, and Roger was staying. She twined her fingers through Roger's. The Christmas Wish Knotts had worked their charm.

Trudy spoke her blessing:

"Je souhaite que l'année nouvelle vous procure bonheur, santé, et prospérité.

"Joyeux Noël, a tous."

Mabel interpreted:

"I wish the new year will bring you happiness, health, and prosperity.

"Merry Christmas, everyone."

Roger squeezed her hand, and she squeezed back. Would this be her new normal? What a perfect gift. Best Christmas present ever. "Stille Nacht" ended, and the room was silent.

The Christmas Ship blared its horn, and everyone turned to the window. The ship blared its horn again, and the room went silent. Everyone gathered at the window, and the lovely notes of "O Holy Night" filled the air. The song ended, and people on the pier cheered, and all the Cliff Edge Condo residents applauded.

Roger lifted her chin, and she melted into him as he took her in his arms and kissed her with a toe-curling, breathtaking kiss. She pulled away and gazed into his eyes. "Are you really staying?"

"I was never going to leave. Not after Cliff Edge Condos stole my heart, or was it you?" He bent down, and she met him halfway, pressing her lips to his. She placed her hands on his solid chest, and his warmth enveloped her like a blanket.

Voices floated across the water singing "Oh Christmas Tree," and the Cliff Edge Condo dwellers added their voices. Sif hummed along as Christmas magic filled the air.

She sighed. All her Christmas wishes had come true. She was in Roger's arms, and he was really staying. She gazed out at the Christmas ship and wished for this night to never end.

A word about the author...

Avis M. Adams lives in the Pacific Northwest and writes poetry, young adult, and middle grade novels. She dabbles in picture books and produces award winning poetry that incorporates the beauty of the region. She is a member of PNWA and was a finalist in the YA and Picture Book categories of their literary contest. She teaches English courses at Green River College, presents at conferences, gardens, and enjoys travel and the great outdoors.

The Incident, her debut YA novel was released in 2021 from The Wild Rose Press. https://avis-m-adams.com